DELHI DISCO

Shikhar Goyal is an iron-and-steel entrepreneur at his day job. He has been educated at St George's College, Mussoorie, University of Delhi, New Delhi and Babson College, USA. Shikhar is passionate about films, photography, public speaking and memes. He runs a blog where he writes slice-of-life articles and also showcases his photography. *Delhi Disco* is Shikhar's first rodeo as an author.

DELHI DISCO

MISCHIEF,

MURDER

& MAYHEM

ON THE DANCE FLOOR

SHIKHAR GOYAL

EBURY
PRESS

An imprint of Penguin Random House

EBURY PRESS

Ebury Press is an imprint of the Penguin Random House group of companies whose addresses can be found at global.penguinrandomhouse.com

Published by Penguin Random House India Pvt. Ltd
4th Floor, Capital Tower 1, MG Road,
Gurugram 122 002, Haryana, India

First published in Ebury Press by Penguin Random House India 2025

Copyright © Shikhar Goyal 2025

All rights reserved

10 9 8 7 6 5 4 3 2 1

ISBN 9780143468479

Typeset in Sabon LT Std by Manipal Technologies Limited, Manipal
Printed at Thomson Press India Ltd, New Delhi

www.penguin.co.in

To all the storytellers out there,
you make the world a tad more interesting

Contents

Prologue

The black Mercedes convertible came to a screeching halt at the traffic light. It was around midnight, and the Delhi air reeked of an earthy smell rising from the wet cement on the pavements. The car's driver stole a quick glance at herself in the rear-view mirror. Her skin looked radiant in the warm red glow cast by the tail lights of other cars at the intersection. Her distinct jawline rested perfectly below her high cheekbones. Yes, the crow's feet around her eyes had become pronounced, but they didn't bother her any more. She was happy with what she saw. She had stopped hiding her age, even though she definitely didn't look it. Women half her age were already making a beeline for Botox clinics and plastic surgeons. But she didn't need that shit. She was better than them. Her disciplined lifestyle had kept her body and mind in shape. In the last twenty years, she had hardly missed a single day's workout. She had already banished carbs from her diet at a time when the rest of the country was years away from discovering the wonders of Keto. She had the superhuman ability to run her staple ten-kilometre route right after a fourteen-hour cross-continental flight, which happened at least twice a month. 'Jet lag is for bozos,' she used to remind her daughter at every instance.

The lights turned green, and she was on her way. She felt energized, despite having had a long day. She had been up since 6 a.m. After a light run and an intense Pilates session, she had dived straight into her business meetings, followed by an interview over lunch with a well-known magazine for their upcoming 'Women in Business' segment. A young chirpy girl with large hipster glasses had conducted the interview.

'Is it fine if I call you Maya?' The girl had asked as the waiter placed a bowl of Caesar salad between them.

'Of course,' Maya had replied, faking sincerity that only a seasoned politician could. Only a privileged few called her directly by her first name. For the rest of the world, she was 'Mrs Kapoor'. Even 'Miss Kapoor' was passable because Mr Kapoor was long dead. And this girl, who looked even younger than her daughter, had the audacity to bypass the social barriers that Maya had carefully constructed around herself.

The interview lasted an hour. Despite the initial faux pas, Maya felt good about this one. To feature in the 'Women in Business' segment meant that she had progressed from being the mere trophy wife she once was to a boardroom bully. Back then, her face was regularly featured on *Delhi Glitz*'s Page 3. She had spent decades in the Delhi party and events circuit. The paparazzi loved her like they loved all good-looking, wealthy women. Maya referred to this as her 'socialite-bimbo phase'.

Now, she wanted to be better known for her business acumen than her fashion sense. Just last month, she had rejected a feature in the 'How to Keep Fit When You Are 55-Plus' segment of a lifestyle magazine (whose name she couldn't remember). Yes, she was on the wrong side of her fifties now. Yes, she could easily pass off as a forty-five-year-old. Yes, she still had her exquisite sense of style. But no, she didn't value being in the public eye any longer. How life changes!

As her car cruised through the bylanes of central Delhi, the silhouette of The Grand Majestic Hotel became larger and clearer, and a sense of comfort eased into her. She was almost home. She couldn't wait to unwind in a hot jacuzzi bath that awaited her in the Presidential Suite, which had been her home for the past two-and-a-half decades. Her car came to a momentary halt at the boom barrier of the hotel, where two well-built guards kept vigil. They recognized their employer and her car within seconds and let her enter the hotel without the customary vehicle inspection that everybody else was subjected to.

The driveway ran for a quarter of a kilometre towards the hotel lobby from the entrance gate. It was covered with manicured plants on both sides. The path went uphill with four hairpin turns, which gave the illusion that the hotel was atop a small mountain. Maya's father-in-law, back in the day, had envisioned the hotel to look like a particular Romanian castle that he had visited during his travels. And voila! The architect had done complete justice to that vision.

Maya stepped out in front of the main entrance lobby with the car's ignition left running behind her. A valet came rushing from his waiting counter and took custody of his employer's beloved car. It was a routine occurrence. Maya would drop her Mercedes in the middle of the porch every night, and she would find it waiting for her there every morning, clean and sparkly, with a full tank.

Upon entering the lobby, she walked past the koi pond with an artificial waterfall and headed straight for the elevators. Once inside, she checked herself out for the second time tonight, this time in front of the full-length elevator mirror. She was a vision of elegance and authority in her crisp blue business suit, the fabric gently hugging her body. A string of white, oval pearls around her neck, and a navy Hermès Birkin clutch in her hands completed the look. The elevator announced her arrival on the twentieth floor with a soft ding. She stepped out and walked through a short corridor before reaching a heavy mahogany door with 'Presidential Suite' written on a plaque next to it.

She tapped the key card against the digital lock, pushing her way into the room. The familiar smell of wild lilies from the hotel room freshener entered her nostrils. Every single day after she left the Presidential Suite for work, it was thoroughly cleaned and prepared by the hotel staff. She came back to a proper and organized home every night. Just the way she liked it.

Her phone buzzed as soon as she kept her clutch down on the table. Her daughter had sent her a text message which read:

There is a problem at Kapital. Need you here!

She sighed. Of course, there was a problem at Kapital! She was naive to think that there was nothing between her and the hot jacuzzi when she had entered the Presidential Suite. But that would have to wait. She would have to go to Kapital, the nightclub she and her husband built, the crown jewel of The Grand Majestic Hotel, and take charge of the situation, whatever it was. That was the price of being a single ambitious woman. Here comes Maya Kapoor to the rescue! Uff!

Exactly four minutes later, she entered Kapital through its gigantic doors, into what was known as the Babylon Bar. The name was a little joke between her and Harsh, her now-deceased husband. In the early days of Kapital, when they were both a pair of young newly married lovers, he had sat her down at a table and said, 'You know what, Maya? I want people to have a sip of alcohol even before they enter our club properly!'

'And how do you propose to do that? Set up a bar right at the entrance?' she had asked with a chuckle.

'Not a bad idea!' he had remarked, and hence Babylon Bar, a small preliminary bar situated at the entrance of the club, had come into existence. It had become an instant hit. But that was years ago.

Today, something seemed off right from the moment Maya stepped in. It was a Saturday night, and the place should have been buzzing with music and people. Instead, it was awfully quiet and there was no sign of anybody there. No bouncers, or 'K Security' as she liked to call them, standing at the entrance to manage the mob of party-goers. No bartenders concocting potent cocktails and quietly fuelling the intensity of the party. No smartly dressed men and women in the mood to let their hair down. Maya's phone buzzed again.

Waiting at the Grand Stage area.

She walked through the dimly lit corridor, which connected the Babylon Bar to the Grand Stage area, where the actual partying happened. The silence felt ominous. A bead of sweat trickled from her forehead down to her face.

Why is the air conditioning off today? she asked herself.

She reached the Grand Stage, which except for the fuzzy moonlight coming through the floor-to-ceiling windows, was enveloped in darkness. Maya switched the flashlight on her phone, but as soon as she did that, she sensed a movement in the darkness, startling her and causing her to drop her phone.

'Who's there? Sameera?' Maya asked out aloud in vain as she crouched to pick up her phone, only to find the flashlight had stopped working.

'Damn it!' she exclaimed when she saw that her phone had gone dead altogether. She was losing her patience.

'Hello? Is anybody here?' she asked into the void.

There was no answer.

'Sameera? What kind of joke is this?' she asked again, frustrated but feigning bravery.

As she started to make a move, the lights came back on, and before she could comprehend what was happening, a bottle of champagne popped and glitter flew all around her.

'Surpriiiiseeee! Happy birthday!' shouted everybody in unison. She saw her daughter and friends cheering happily for her. There was more laughter and noise until somebody noticed the colour fade from the birthday girl's face as she fell on the floor with her hand firmly placed on the left part of her chest. The surprise birthday party quickly turned into a horror show as the last thing Maya saw was a haze of chaotic frenzy and blinding disco lights, followed by nothing at all.

Five Years Later

1

Homecoming of Sorts

'First time in India, eh?' the immigration officer asked Neil after quickly studying his blank passport pages. A transparent glass wall separated them both.

'First time anywhere outside the United States of America, sir,' said Neil, forcing a smile so that this interaction could finish quickly. It had been an eighteen-hour non-stop flight from New York City to New Delhi, and he was jittery from all the time he had spent wrestling the craving for a cigarette. The temptation to quickly puff on his electronic vape in the flight washroom had presented itself several times during the flight, but he was iffy about flouting international rules and regulations on his first-ever trip abroad. The plan was hence dropped.

'So, what brings you to India?' asked the immigration officer, who seemed to be in a rather chatty mood.

'Two reasons, actually. I am here for work and also to surprise my girlfriend. She lives in Delhi,' replied Neil.

'Ah! Love makes men do extreme things like travelling across continents! Look at the camera on your right. Chin slightly up. I remember when I was in my youth I was very wild myself. I often climbed up to the third floor of the building to sneak into my girlfriend's room!' said the officer with pride and absolutely no urgency as a sea of red-eyed passengers queued up behind Neil.

'What a great story, sir!' said Neil, stuck in a dilemma—to either punch the officer in the face or play it safe by making small talk with him. He decided on the latter.

'Put both your thumbs on the green machine and press. So, you were born and brought up in America itself?' the officer asked.

'Yes, sir. A citizen of the United States through and through. Born in Boston. Raised in Boston. And making a living in New York City,' said Neil, providing information, most of which anybody should be able to figure out by looking at his passport.

'All of you Indians in America make my heart swell with pride. Now, put your right hand and press. People like Satya Nadella and Sundar Pichai are ruling the world and putting India right there on the world map!' the officer chimed in with joy.

'That is true sir! Indians are doing a brilliant job everywhere,' replied Neil, waiting for this ordeal to end so that he could be on his way.

'Left hand now. So, tell me, Mr Ramamurthy! Are you a software engineer or a future business mogul?' asked the officer, his excitement palpable in his overflowing belly.

'Neither, sir,' replied Neil.

'Oh, then a doctor perhaps? You know my older son just cleared his . . .'

'I'm just a DJ, sir!' interrupted Neil, regretting his decision not to punch the officer.

'A what? DJ?' the bemused officer expressed his unfamiliarity with the term.

'Yes, sir! DJ. A disc-jockey. I play music in clubs,' replied Neil.

'Oh!' said the officer in disbelief. 'So, your work visa isn't to run a start-up here?'

'No sir,' said Neil, handing him a bunch of papers. 'It is to play music at a few clubs. Here are the sponsorship letters.'

Neil had shattered the officer's expectation of another Indian-origin person bringing glory to the country. Neil's passport was promptly stamped, and he was set free without any further conversation. Even though Neil wanted to protest and put forth the pros of his profession, the magical anticipation of putting a smooth white stick of tobacco between his lips was overpowering.

The smoking lounge was small and crammed with men mostly. Neil felt an instant rush of euphoria when the first wave of smoke entered his windpipe and into his lungs. With two more drags, he felt the jitters disappearing, his nerves becoming calmer and his mind, clearer. By the time he was on his third cigarette, his phone rang. It was his mother: 'Landed safely?'

'Yes, Maa,' he replied.

'Good! Did you clear immigration yet?' she asked.

'Yes, it was a breeze,' he replied and chuckled to himself.

'Good! I hope that the ring is safe and sound?' It was more of a question than a statement.

Neil felt the small ring box in the pocket of his cargo pants and replied, 'Yes, Maa! The ring is safe with me. I carried it on me throughout the flight.'

'Good! Don't lose it. When your father proposed to me with that ring thirty years ago, it changed our lives. Now, it is yours to give to my future daughter-in-law.'

'Yes, I know, Maa. Don't worry!' replied Neil as he took a drag of his cigarette.

'Okay, you take care now. My students are waiting for me. I'll talk to you soon. Bye.'

'Bye, Maa! Love you!' Neil answered back.

'And Neil, one more thing!' his Maa said.

'Yeah?'

'Try to smoke a little less while you are in India.'

'Yes, Maa,' Neil said as he took another puff.

The hot polluted air of Delhi slapped him in the face as he came out of the airport, pushing a luggage trolley in front of him. The weather was very different from the air-conditioned indoors. One thing was for sure—all those reports about Delhi's air quality index were not exaggerated. As Neil pushed the trolley a little further on to the main road, he came across a series of billboards on the other side of the road. Sandwiched between the ads of iPhone 16 Pro and Audi Q5, was an oddly familiar ad. Its background was all glossy black. A shiny golden disco ball adorned the billboard at its center. Below it, in a cursive ornate font were the words:

Delhi's Capital of Dance and Music
Reopening on Saturday, 12 April, 2025.
Kapital—The Club,
20th Floor, The Grand Majestic Hotel, New Delhi.

Neil felt a tap on his shoulder. He turned around to see a man in a khaki shirt–pant combo, chewing a blood-red leafy substance in his mouth, which definitely did not look like chewing gum.

'Looking for a taxi, sir?' he asked, as he spat the contents of his mouth out on the road. 'Very cheap taxi!'

'As a matter of fact, I am looking for one,' replied Neil, his voice reeking of a thick American accent.

'Great! Let me take you to your destination,' said the over-eager driver, taking immediate charge of Neil's luggage trolley. 'Where you want to go? Noida? Gurgaon? Ghaziabad? I go everywhere!'

Neil pointed at the black billboard behind him and said, 'The Grand Majestic Hotel.'

'Rs 5000 only. Discounted price for you, my friend,' said the man without thinking twice.

Neil ran the numbers in his head, converting the rupee value into dollars, and once satisfied, said, 'Let's go!'

Neil had seen big chandeliers. But this particular one that hovered over his head was humongous. He wondered if the singular metal chain that held it were to snap into two, would his head then be strewn around the lobby of The Grand Majestic Hotel in multiple places? Maybe that's why the dapper elderly gentleman, dressed in a tailored waistcoat, sitting at the grand piano and playing soothing jazz, had set himself up far away from the chandelier.

'Mr Ramamurthy, here is your passport. And this is your room key card. Your room number is 5023,' said the concierge to Neil, ending his morbid chain of thought.

'Thank you so much, Divya,' said Neil, reading her name tag and collecting both the items handed to him.

'Our staff will bring your luggage directly to your room. I hope you have a grand stay with us,' said Divya, a dazzling toothpaste-commercial smile plastered on her face.

'Uh, Divya? Could you help me with a matter, please?' ventured Neil. A psychologist on Instagram had once advocated that it was best to call people by their first names before asking for a favour. Rapport building, he had called it. Time to test that theory.

'Absolutely, sir! I'll be glad to assist you with anything you want!' she replied.

'You see, I am an old friend of your boss, Miss Sameera Kapoor. I flew in especially from the United States to surprise her. Could you tell me where I could find her?'

'Umm, Miss Kapoor . . . I don't know . . .'

Divya, who had been fluent so far, began stuttering at the mention of her boss. Neil had asked her something completely out of the concierge training syllabus.

'Well? Divya?' asked Neil.

'Sir, I am not privy to Miss Kapoor's schedule. I'm afraid that I won't be of much help in that regard,' she said, regaining some of that lost fluency. Time to unfollow the psychologist on Instagram.

'All right No stress. But would you happen to know if she is at the hotel today?' asked Neil.

'I am sorry, sir, but I do not have that information. Is there anything else that I can assist you with?' she asked, wanting to excuse herself from this conversation and probably tend to those guests who were more likely to enquire about the best way to reach the Qutab Minar than the ones who wanted to know her boss' whereabouts.

'Well, I could write my number down for you. In case you spot Sameera at the hotel, please let me know?' asked Neil, not wanting to give up so easily.

'Sir, I am not allowed to take down personal contact details of our guests for non-official purposes. But you could perhaps speak to Mr Singh,' she told him.

'Mr Singh?'

'Yes. Mr Gyan Singh, Miss Kapoor's PA. He might be able to help you out,' Divya said, scanning the hotel lobby behind Neil.

'And where can I find this Mr Gyan Singh, Divya?' asked Neil, excited that he had finally made some breakthrough.

'He is over there,' she said, pointing towards a man reading the *Times of India* on the single-seater sofa. 'Grey safari suit.'

'Okay, thank you so much!' said Neil, his eyes fixated in Gyan Singh's direction.

Neil, with Divya in tow, walked towards the enigmatic man in the grey safari suit whose face was buried deep inside the newspaper. As they approached closer to him, Gyan Singh's imposing physicality became obvious. He was tall even while sitting down. According to Neil's analysis, he must be at least 6'4" or 6'5". His arms and shoulders were well-defined and very muscular. He looked more like a bodyguard than a PA.

'Mr Singh?' stuttered Divya. 'Mr Gyan . . . Singh?'

The man calmly looked up from the newspaper. His head was trimmed into a perfect crew cut as if he had just come out of the barber's shop. He sported a thick handlebar moustache and had a resting angry face.

'Yes?' Mr Singh asked in a heavy voice.

'This gentleman here wants to meet Ms Kapoor. He says that he is her friend from the United States,' Divya told Gyan Singh.

'Mr Singh, hi!' Neil chimed in immediately before Gyan Singh had time to process anything. 'My name is Neil Ramamurthy. I have come from the United States to meet your boss, Miss Kapoor. Can you tell me where I can find her?'

Gyan Singh waited for a torturous two seconds before replying.

'Why do you want to meet Boss Madam?'

'I am her boyfriend. Well, ex-boyfriend actually. It is a bit complicated, really. I should say that we are good friends since we are taking a break from active dating. I hope you follow my drift,' said Neil as the big bulky man tried to make sense of the information dumped on him by an Indian dude with an American accent.

Mr Singh's height was evident when he kept his newspaper aside and stood up. Neil tilted his neck uncomfortably to look up at him.

'You said "boyfriend"? Are you Boss Madam's boyfriend?' Gyan Singh had singled the B-word out.

'Yes and no. It is a bit complicated. Let me explain . . .'

'Yes or no?' asked Gyan Singh, not giving Neil a chance to elaborate, while Divya regretted her decision to introduce both parties.

'We dated for a few months before taking a break because she had to move back to India. You know how it is with girls,' Neil tried to explain to him.

'This does not make any sense to me,' said Gyan Singh bluntly. 'I am going to call Boss Madam on her phone and confirm this. If this wild story of yours is even 1 per cent fake, I am going to personally escort you out of the premises.'

'But, but . . . Mr Singh if you could simply take me to Sameera without calling her first, that would be great. I flew eighteen hours non-stop to surprise her. Please don't ruin the surprise,' said Neil, his hands folded in sincere prayer.

But the request landed on deaf ears as Gyan Singh had already taken his cell phone, an old-school Nokia, out and pressed the necessary buttons. In the era of touchscreen smartphones, Gyan Singh's phone seemed like a rebellious outcast.

Gyan Singh moved out of Neil's earshot and had a brief conversation on the phone. After he was done, he came back to Neil and told him, 'Boss Madam wants to meet you.'

'That is awesome!' exclaimed Neil, resisting the urge to hi-five this unusually tall man because he knew that it wouldn't be reciprocated. 'Where is she?'

'Top floor. At the club,' replied Mr Singh.

Divya heaved a sigh of relief and went back to her work as usual. A man dressed in all-white, sitting behind Gyan Singh, eavesdropped on the entire conversation.

2

Shrimp Cocktail

'OH MY GOD, NEIIILLL!' Sameera was ecstatic. 'It really is you!' she said as she put aside her wine and stood up on the toes in her neon green Balenciagas to embrace him in a bear hug.

'It is me, in the flesh! Just the way you last saw me!' said Neil as an army of half-a-dozen odd employees of Sameera looked on. All of them wore blue polo T-shirts which had the letter 'K' embossed in black on their pockets. Sameera wore the same t-shirt except that her 'K' was golden.

'Oh my god! Oh my god! I thought Gyan Singh was joking when he mentioned your name,' said Sameera, not letting him go after the hug, which Neil didn't mind in the slightest.

'I am sorry to interrupt your meeting like this,' said Neil as her employees stared at him, the intruder who had just hijacked their precious time with the boss.

'Oh! Come on! It is super chill. I was just wrapping things up anyway,' she said. 'By the way, this is my team to kickstart Kapital 2.0. The opening party is this Saturday!'

'Oh right! I saw a giant billboard for Kapital just outside the airport! It was hard to miss,' he said. 'How are the preparations coming along?'

'Fan-tastic!' she said, breaking the word into two for emphasis. 'Everything is just fan-tastic! We are just ironing out the minor details before the event.'

'Ma'am!' A girl in a blue T-shirt with braces in her teeth and a writing pad in her hands called out to Sameera. 'Which champagne flutes should we finalize for the party?'

'Neil darling, just give me two seconds, please. Let me finish this!' said Sameera.

'Absolutely. Don't hold yourself back on my account,' said Neil, taking a subtle step backwards.

'Show me both the flutes,' asserted Sameera to the girl, and instantaneously a boy in blue t-shirt appeared with two almost identical champagne glasses and duly submitted them to his boss.

The girl with the writing pad spoke up. 'Ma'am, the flute on the left is from LSA International, manufactured in the United Kingdom. The flute on the right is Japanese, made by Kimura Glass. Both are very durable and highly recommended by our vendors.'

Sameera analysed both glasses closely, holding them each in her hands one by one and doing a complete 360° inspection.

'Umm Neil, what do you think? Which flute will go better for our party?' she asked.

'I think the one on the right will make a sick impression. It is a no-brainer for me!' said Neil, who couldn't tell them apart even if his life depended on it.

'Yes! I was thinking the same. Let us go with the one on the right.' Sameera informed her employee.

'Sure ma'am,' she said and dispersed around the club with the rest of the staff.

'Look at you! Being a boss and leader to these people,' said Neil when nobody else was in their earshot.

'Very funny,' said Sameera, playfully smacking him on the back of his head.

'I am not joking! Your staff looks up to you. I could see it in their eyes. Especially that human giant, your PA, Mr Singh, with whom I am already acquainted. He is built more like a bodyguard if you ask me!' said Neil, looking in the direction of Mr Singh who had accompanied him to the club, and now stood quietly with his hands folded at the gigantic entrance door.

'Oh, Gyan Singh is harmless! He only looks scary and intimidating but he is the most resourceful person on my payroll. A very loyal man. He has been with my family before I was born,' said Sameera.

'I don't doubt that at all. The man is ancient. Still uses a Nokia, a non-smartphone! Can you even imagine?' said Neil, making a mind-blown gesture with his hands.

'Enough about him,' said Sameera protectively of Gyan Singh. 'You tell me! How come you are in India all of a sudden? Still couldn't get over me?' Sameera teased him.

'Oh, I am one hundred per cent over you, all right?' said Neil, the weight of the ring heavier than before in his cargo pants.

'Good! Because that boat has sailed already,' she said, making a friendly yet firm statement.

'Yes, I know! I am not a naïve little kid,' he said, shrugging his shoulders. 'I am actually here in Delhi because I have landed a bunch of DJing gigs in some clubs. Here, check this list out. You might know of some of these places already,' said Neil as he handed his phone to Sameera.

Sameera went through the list and exclaimed, 'Wow! These are literally ALL of my competitors, Neil! There is Blue Mushroom, Paradiso, Lucky Loser, MOQA and others! I don't know whether I should be impressed or envious!'

'I'll take that as a compliment, thank you! I have been actively sending out my mixes to these clubs in the past few months. Some of them reverted, offering me some trial slots. So here I am, going around the Delhi disco circuit for a month,' said Neil.

'Then back to New York?' asked Sameera, trying hard to conceal her disappointment.

'New York or somewhere else. I don't know,' answered Neil with both palms in the air. 'I am yet to hear back from clubs in Bengaluru, Mumbai, Bangkok and Seoul. Let's see where life takes me.'

'Well, as long as you are in Delhi, why don't you play for Kapital as well? I can put in a good word with the owner,' said Sameera, blinking an eye.

'Oh, you don't say!' said Neil, and the both of them laughed at that.

'Come on, let me show you around the club,' said Sameera, as she began walking in front and gestured for him to follow behind her. 'Feel free to give your input since you have literally lived half your life in clubs. You can act as my consultant for now. But mind you, I won't give you a single penny for services rendered.'

'Don't worry, ma'am. Money is not an issue for me. I can do it pro bono,' retorted Neil for which he received a light punch to his stomach.

Sameera held his hand and began the tour. 'This is Babylon, the first bar of the club,' she said, pointing towards a counter in front of a wall, stocked with numerous exotic alcohol bottles from around the world.

'Wow!' said Neil. 'This is quite a collection!'

'Wait till you see the Olympus, the main bar!' Sameera remarked smugly.

'Wait, what? This isn't the main bar?' asked Neil, visibly confused.

'No, this is just the warm-up bar. You know, just to get people started,' said Sameera without further elaboration. 'Come, I'll now take you to the Grand Stage area which *you* particularly will find interesting.'

'Let's go!'

Sameera led him through a dark corridor lit only by tiny blue lights scattered like stars in the night sky. Towards the end, they were greeted by a flickering signboard that read: **'Good Time to have a Good Time.'** And upon crossing it, they entered a hall of massive proportions. In the middle was an elevated stage for the DJ and all around it was the dance floor. On two out of the four perimetric walls, there was a display of the largest alcohol collection that Neil had ever seen in his life. Olympus, the main bar! There was every bottle and every brand that was known to Neil, and more. Babylon was indeed the warm-up bar.

'Sameera, Olympus is beautiful!' Neil said, his eyes wide open in pure unadulterated amazement.

'Thank you,' said Sameera joyfully. 'Also, check out the DJ stage. It is right in the centre so that people can dance all around it! A complete 360 degrees experience!'

'The stage is just insane, Sam! Your club will do wonders! I can feel it in my veins,' said Neil in all sincerity.

'Thank you! The credit actually goes to my parents, who were the OG visionaries of their time; the true pioneers of the party scene in Delhi,' said Sameera proudly.

'Come on! Look at the work that you are doing. You deserve the credit too,' said Neil.

'Nah! I just gave this place a bit of a touch-up really. It had been lying dormant ever since that night when Mom . . .' Sameera found herself unable to finish the sentence. But she didn't have to. Neil had heard the tragic story of her Mom's surprise birthday party when they had started dating.

Neil hugged her lightly from the side and said, 'Hey, hey! It's all right. Don't worry, your parents will be proud of you for the work that you have put in.'

Sameera recovered from her emotions and said, 'Come on, Let's check out the rest of the club.'

She showed him around the premises, whizzing through numerous iterations of light and sound checks. Neil saw that the team of the blue polo T-shirt staff was significantly bigger than the one he saw initially. There were several of them, scattered around the club in groups of twos and threes, armed with walkie-talkies, writing pads, and a strong sense of purpose for their respective tasks.

'And last but not least, this is the kitchen,' said Sameera as she opened a double swinging door and ushered Neil inside. Like everything else at the club, the kitchen too was spread out to cover an expansive area. There were counters for cutting and chopping, stations for cooking, frying, baking and mixing and lots and lots of storage space.

'I must have been to a hundred odd clubs in my life. But I have never seen a kitchen this massive. As your newly appointed club consultant, it is my duty to tell you that spending shitloads of money on a kitchen like this does not make financial sense,' said Neil with a pretend sense of authority, and not being able to resist adding a cheeky comment afterwards. 'People come to clubs to dance and drink and not to eat and excrete.'

'Eww, Neil! Who talks about excretion and that too in the kitchen?' Sameera immediately retorted, making a disgusted face. 'We have a proper kitchen at Kapital because we strive to be different. We want our patrons to keep coming back for the excellent food apart from the wonderful party experience. The food is our USP.'

'What is this talk that I hear about the legitimacy of my kitchen?' asked a man walking into the scene from the far end of the kitchen. He was shorter than Neil, middle-aged, and wore a complete chef's white uniform from top to bottom.

'Hello, Chef Alex! I was expecting to bump into you in the kitchen,' said Sameera, not surprised by his sudden appearance.

'Good afternoon, Miss Kapoor!" said the chef, bending in a slight bow. "I had just finished preparing the tasting menu for your opening party,'

'Fan-tastic! I cannot wait to try the hors d'oeuvres!' Sameera's excitement was palpable. 'Neil, you will love them!'

'And who is this gentleman that I have not been introduced to yet?' Chef Alex asked before Neil had a chance to reply to Sameera.

'Oh, this is Neil! He is my friend from the States,' said Sameera, as Neil smiled through the soul-crushing sting of the word 'friend'. 'And Neil, this is Chef Alex Matthews, the head chef at Saba, the fine dining restaurant on the first floor of the hotel. You would have probably seen the name in the elevator. Chef Alex is quite the celebrity in Delhi. His restaurant accounts for half the traffic at the hotel! His team is going to be handling Kapital's kitchen as well.'

'Wow! I have never met an Indian celebrity before!' exclaimed Neil, offering his hand forward. 'It is a pleasure to meet you, chef'

'Nice to meet you too, mister,' said Chef Alex, shaking his hand. 'But sorry to disappoint you, I am no celebrity. Miss Kapoor is too kind and generous with her compliments.'

'Ah! Chef Alex, ever so modest!' remarked Sameera. 'Neil, wait till you try the shrimp cocktail. You will know that my compliments are not exaggerated.'

'Your wish is my command, Miss Kapoor,' said Chef Alex, as he started walking towards the other side of the kitchen, away from their earshot.

'You have celebrity staff on your roaster. I am impressed, Miss Kapoor,' teased Neil.

'He is a celebrity, all right!' Sameera emphasized. 'He has appeared as a guest judge in a few episodes of

Master Baker and *Gourmet Chef India*. That is a big deal!'

'Indeed, it is,' said Neil as he saw Chef Alex walking towards them balancing two small cocktail glasses on a tray in his hands.

'Voila!' said Chef Alex, proudly presenting his creation to the both of them.

'Go on, try it, milady.'

Sameera picked the glass closest to her and took a bite. 'Oh my god! Chef, you have outdone yourself this time!' she declared, her eyes closed in euphoria while she savoured the delicacy.

'You should also try it,' said Alex to Neil. 'I want to know what you think of it!'

Neil picked the only glass left in front of him and put the shrimp cocktail reluctantly in his mouth as the chef and his ex-girlfriend looked on. He wasn't big on seafood, but he couldn't disappoint Sameera. The immediate taste wasn't so bad. It got better as he chewed on. He hated to admit, but it was actually delicious. Maybe he should change his stance on seafood after all. God! He had forgotten how hungry he was! He had last eaten on the flight about three hours ago. As soon as he had gulped down the shrimp cocktail, he wanted to ask for more, but somehow the words wouldn't come out of his mouth. They were there as clear as day in his head: 'Can I have another one, please?' However, his voice failed to vocalize a single alphabet. It was a strange feeling. He cleared

his throat a little and tried again. Same result. He
cleared his throat a little more vigorously this time and
opened his mouth to speak. But instead of words, thick
greenish-yellow bile escaped his mouth. Neil threw up
on the kitchen floor as Sameera looked on cluelessly
and in horror, and Chef Alex took a step backwards
so as to protect his squeaky-clean black shoes from
getting smudged.

3

Creatures of the Night

'HE FLEW ALL THE WAY FROM New York?' It was more of a remark than a question. Emily's voice echoed throughout the Presidential Suite from Sameera's iPad while a speaker played 'Drive By' by Train in the background.

'He did!' Sameera, sitting cross-legged on the couch, found herself blushing from ear to ear.

'Sam, why don't you marry him already?' Emily pestered her. 'If a man flew across continents and oceans to be with me, I would marry him in an instant. I swear!'

'Well, he's not exactly here to be with me,' Sameera told her. 'He has landed some DJ gigs in Delhi. Once he wraps those up, he'll be off to another city.'

Emily stared silently at Sameera for two seconds leading the latter to believe that there was a glitch on her iPad screen.

'Babe, are you even listening to yourself?' asked Emily finally after the one-sided stare-off. Sameera shrugged her shoulders, annoyed that her best friend was going to throw a truth bomb at her.

'Okay so let me narrate your entire love story to you from the beginning because it seems to me that your dementia is back again,' said Emily.

'I know my story! You don't need to narrate it,' Sameera protested, but she knew that there was no winning against Emily.

'So, you land in New York City to do a short eight-week executive course in business management over the icy cold winters. You match with a cute guy on Hinge and meet him at a coffee shop. The date goes well, and you make plans to meet at a club in two days. However, this time, the boy ghosts you. You are sitting at the bar, nursing a heartbreak cocktail in your hands, when the club's DJ, who is also a cute guy, if I may add, dedicates a song "to the cute girl who shouldn't be sitting by herself at the bar". It is a song that you love. You guys end up talking later that night. He asks you out on a proper date for later that week. You agree. You have a good time. You guys go for a couple more dates. And soon you guys are officially dating. The DJ boy is hopelessly head over heels in love with you. On your seventh week anniversary, which also happens to be New Year's Eve, he takes you to Times Square, where he has arranged for a full-blown orchestra with violins and whatnot! He then gets down on his knees and proposes to you with his mother's wedding ring as a crowd of thousands cheers him on. You reject his proposal and break his heart. You fly back to India after your course is over. A couple of months later, the DJ boy is in Delhi as a surprise and is staying at your hotel. He tells you that he is here for a DJ gig in Delhi. Tell me, if I got anything wrong so far?' asked Emily at the end of her monologue.

'It is all correct, so far,' admitted Sameera. She was well accustomed to Emily's memory and capacity for monologues.

'Sam, do you seriously believe all this to be a coincidence? Neil is here to win you back, stupid! If this is not true love, I don't know what it is!'

'Honestly, Emily, I am a bit overwhelmed with the opening of Kapital right now. I don't have time for love,' said Sameera.

'Yes, I know that you are a busy businesswoman with a mission to crack the *Forbes* '30 Under 30' list, and you have a little under three years to accomplish that. But mark my words, *all* the good guys will be taken if you wait that long.' said Emily, putting an extra emphasis on 'all.'

'I hear you, Em! But I gotta do what I gotta do,' said Sameera and shrugged at the iPad screen. 'God bless the day I met you as an exchange student in Canada. You know me better than I know myself.'

'Oh, that I do,' said Emily, chugging her remaining cup of steaming hot latte in one sip. 'On that note, I will have to take your leave now. It is almost noon, here in Vancouver, and I must return to my soul-crushing corporate job.'

'Go seize the day, bestie! I'll catch you next week, same time?' asked Sameera.

'Wouldn't miss it for the world!' said Emily and waved her best friend across the globe goodbye.

It was half past one in Sameera's time zone. It was time to sleep.

Neil's stomach was still acting funny. He shouldn't have had the shrimp cocktail in the first place. He should have known that his American stomach was too sensitive to handle food in India. Today had been the worst possible start of his endeavor to win back his ex-girlfriend. But the more pressing issue right now was to set the thermostat at the exact correct temperature. One degree lower and it was too cold. One degree higher, and the heat would ensure that he was sweating and twisting and turning in his bed. And to add to his sorrows, the thermostat did not speak Fahrenheit. Only Celsius. He could Google a conversion chart, but laziness got the better of him. Phew! The only solution that seemed plausible was to pop a melatonin tablet. That would definitely put him to sleep for the next eight hours or so irrespective of the room's temperature.

As he lay in bed after washing the pill down his throat with a full glass of water, his phone chimed with a WhatsApp message notification. It was a special tone set for a particular contact. He knew exactly who the texter was and had a very strong hunch about what the message was going to be. Reluctantly, he opened his phone and confirmed the hunch.

(Maa) Did she say 'yes?'
(Neil) I did not ask her yet, Maa
(Maa) What's the delay? Is she dating anybody in India already?
Neil)) No, Maa!
(Maa) Then what is the delay?
(Neil) I am not sure if she is dating somebody or not

His mother did not type anything even though a small badge under her contact indicated that she was online.

(Neil) Maa? Are you there?
(Maa) I am just worried for you, *beta*. I don't want your trip to be all for nothing. You have worked so hard for this
(Neil) Don't worry, Maa. I am going to be fine. I am going to win her back. I know it in my heart
(Maa) Yes, of course you will. You are capable of anything that you set your heart to!
(Neil) I love you, Maa. I miss you :*
(Maa) I love you too, *beta*!

(Neil) Talk to you tomorrow? I am a little tired
(Maa) Okay, bye! Goodnight! Make sure you have
a good breakfast after waking up! Your body needs
proper nutrition after all that travel.

Before he could tell her that his nutrition had already
gone for a toss earlier today, he was already snoring
soundly with his phone lying on his chest.

The kettle let out a generous steam of vapours to let the
man in the apartment know that the water was now
piping hot. The man, wearing a pair of chequered boxers
and a bathing robe, picked the kettle carefully from the
handle and poured its contents into an opened box of cup
noodles. He went a little over the top of the prescribed
mark in the box. He had discovered that the noodles
tasted infinitely better when they were a little extra soupy.
Dry noodles were for sociopaths who did not know food.

He then poured himself a glass of red wine into
a plastic tumbler and settled himself into the couch.
He pressed play on the remote and the 102-inch LED
TV screen came to life in front of him. A war episode
of *Vikings*, which he had watched fifty times already,
started playing. He loved everything about the show.
The beautiful landscapes, the free-spirited and well-
endowed women, the violence . . . Oh, the violence!
There was something really peaceful and soothing

about watching people crack each other's skulls open. He could watch this episode over and over again. It was oddly therapeutic.

The doorbell rang. Who could it be at this time? It was a little past midnight. A little annoyed and a little curious, he got up from his couch and went to get the door. The peephole showed a man standing outside in a red T-shirt and a red cap. Probably a delivery boy looking for directions.

'What do you want?' he asked the delivery boy as he opened the door.

'This is for you, sir,' said the delivery boy, holding a tub of Ben & Jerry's Chocolate Chip ice cream in front of him.

'I did not order this!' the man barked at him.

'Are you Alex Matthews? And is this apartment number 607?' asked the delivery boy.

'I am and this is,' replied Alex.

'Then this is for you. This is a gift, sir. There is a note also attached,' said the delivery boy, referring to the small chit of paper placed on the ice cream tub.

'Read it aloud,' demanded Alex.

Dear Alex,

This dessert is for the sweetest person in my life!

Love,
Sameera.

A smiling Alex collected the ice cream and shut the door behind him leaving the hopeful delivery boy devoid of any tips. He got back onto his cozy couch and resumed the *Vikings*. One by one he would devour the holy trifecta of his late-night food binge: the cup noodles, the red wine and the ice cream. Perfect.

There was an alert on his phone from Zomato. It read:

> Sameera, your order of Ben & Jerry's Chocolate Chip ice cream was successfully delivered. Thank you for choosing Zomato. Please rate the delivery experience.

Alex smiled and kept the phone down. Until Sameera sends him a midnight dessert delivery, he would continue sending them to himself on her behalf. One-sided love is a bitch. Anyway, somebody just got their eyes gouged out on the TV. It was going to be a fun night.

4

My Club, My Rules

The glitz. The glamour. The glimmer. The shimmer. The opening night party at Kapital was straight out of a red-carpet Bollywood event. The who's-who of Delhi had turned up donning designer gowns and tuxedos. Champagne flutes were passed around and clinked as everybody cheered for the reopening of the city's party capital after a hiatus of five years.

While Sameera played the perfect hostess to the throng of guests pouring into her club, Neil found himself standing next to Gyan Singh, Sameera's PA and Divya, the hotel concierge, at the Babylon Bar. Gyan Singh, clad in a navy-blue safari suit, stood alert and impassive, watching the night unravel with keen, military alertness. Divya, still in her duty colours and holding on loosely to a clipboard, tapped along to the pulsating beats of the club.

'So, are you both enjoying the party?' Neil asked them, an attempt at small talk.

'Yes,' said Divya instantly.

'What?' asked Gyan Singh, looking down at Neil from his towering height.

'I asked whether you are having a good time?' said Neil, a notch louder this time for the convenience of the giraffe.

'No enjoyment on duty,' said Gyan Singh dryly, causing Divya to suppress a chuckle.

'You should loosen up a bit,' said Neil. 'Let yourself flow with the beats. You get my drift? Even my mother says, "All work and no play makes Neil a dull boy."'

'I work for Boss Madam, not your mother,' said Gyan Singh. Divya turned in the other direction to release a silent laugh.

'Okay, chill chill homie,' said Neil. 'Let's not get personal here.'

'What are you guys talking about?'

It was Sameera. She had come from behind, wearing a one-piece golden dress and carrying two flutes of champagne with her. She handed one to Neil, who took her aside, away from Gyan Singh's hearing radius.

'That Frankenstein's monster of yours is a tough nut to crack,' he told her.

Sameera burst out laughing.

'And that is precisely why he is so efficient at his job,' she said.

'And what is his job exactly? I've not been able to get a grip on that question ever since I set foot at your Grand Majestic Hotel five days ago,' said Neil.

'Go figure!' scoffed Sameera.

Divya came to Sameera and showed her some information on the clipboard, which Sameera quickly went through and dismissed her.

'So, about Gyan Singh,' said Neil after Divya left. 'Do you think he owns a wardrobe of full safari suits in every colour possible?'

'It is the opening night of my club, Neil! Can we please not discuss my employee right now? God!' said Sameera, visibly exasperated.

'Understood, *Boss Madam*,' said Neil, and before Sameera could react, he quickly gulped the entire champagne down. 'By the way, your party is a roaring success. Look at those happy faces all around Kapital!'

'Flattery is a nice way of saving your ass, Mr Ramamurthy,' said Sameera, as she took his arm, locked in with hers and started walking towards the Grand Stage tunnel. 'Come on, it is high time that I had some fun at my own party!'

The tunnel corridor was teeming with party-goers and engulfed in a thick fog of e-cigarette smoke. Sameera led Neil to the other end where a photographer and his team were busy clicking pictures of the guests against the designated photo booth wall.

'Come on, let's get clicked! These pictures will feature in *Delhi Glitz* tomorrow!' Sameera told Neil and dragged him to the front of the photo booth as other people looked on.

'But aren't we supposed to get in the queue?' protested Neil by the time the photographer had already clicked a bunch of their pictures.

'My club. My rules,' Sameera told him as they exited the tunnel passageway and entered the Grand Stage area.

The party pulsated with energy. A flood of moving bodies swayed to the beats spun by the DJ who was clad in black jeans, a plain white tee and stylish sunglasses. Above, the disco lights flickered in a mesmerizing array of colours, intensifying the ambience of the dance floor. Meanwhile, at Olympus, the main bar, mixologists crafted and served an endless procession of cocktails to a steady stream of eager guests.

'Do you want another drink, Neil?' Sameera asked. 'Or chuck that. Let's just go dance!'

'You seem tipsy, Sam!' he told her.

'Ten points to Gryffindor for correctly guessing my current level of drunkenness! Are you going to join me on the dance floor or not?'

Neil did not keep Sameera in suspense. With a big eager smile on his face, he followed Sameera to the dance floor.

Chef Alex barked orders at his army of sous chefs, line cooks, washers and cleaners like they were preparing for war in the kitchen.

'Ravi! Where are we with the sliders? At this rate, all the bread will turn into brick!' he yelled, invoking fear in his subordinates.

'Coming right up, che . . . chef!' said Ravi, stuttering under the high-pressure environment.

Chef Alex moved around the aisles and observed everything minutely. The smallest instance of negligence would be used as a grenade to destroy some poor worker's morale.

'Chop! Chop! Javed!' he told a junior chef who was cutting onions. 'You need to go longer and thinner on these!'

The kitchen door opened and in walked two waiters carrying a tray each of empty dishes and giggling amongst themselves.

'What is the joke? Let me on it too?' growled Chef Alex at them.

The two young waiters swallowed their giggles and made a face solemn enough for a funeral.

'Come on! You can tell me! How's the party going on outside?' asked Chef Alex, his tone uncomfortably friendly all of a sudden.

'We were just discussing how the party is turning out to be a success! And everybody is praising the food,' said one of the waiters.

'That is believable because my food is the bloody best in the world!' exclaimed Chef Alex.

'It is . . . it is indeed, sir!'

'How did Miss Kapoor like the food?' Alex enquired further. 'Did you serve the sliders to her as instructed?'

'We did try, chef, but she told us that she wasn't hungry,' said the waiter.

'She was more in a drink-and-dance kind of a mood, chef,' said the other waiter, who had been quiet so far. He had averted a possible volcanic eruption with his timely input, given the amount of emphasis the chef had given them to serve Miss Kapoor before the party began.

'Is that so? Shall I take the sliders to her myself?' asked Alex.

The waiters did not answer because there was no telling whether their boss was being sarcastic.

'Miss Kapoor had specially placed them on the menu. Where is she exactly in the club right now?' Chef Alex asked.

'She is on the dance floor, dancing with her boyfriend from America!' replied the first waiter.

'Boyfriend? Why do you say boyfriend? They are friends!' said the chef, his voice becoming more menacing with each syllable.

'They are dancing very closely, chef. I thought that they are . . .' said the waiter, a thick bead of sweat appearing on his forehead.

'Okay fine, both of you get back to work. The onion rings are ready for serving,' Alex dismissed them. Both the waiters made themselves scarce as soon as possible without saying a word.

Alex pretended to take another round of the kitchen. After he was done, he marched out into the club still wearing his chef whites. The club was packed to the hilt, and it was difficult to spot Sameera. He was able to locate her after a few minutes. She was on the dance floor just in front of the DJ stage. And true to the intel, she was slow dancing while being locked in a deep embrace with that American skidmark, Neil Ramamurthy.

5

Of Heartbreaks and Louis Vuittons

'I think I am a little drunk,' said Sameera, her arms around his neck while Neil had his wrapped hands around her waist.

'That makes the two of us!' replied Neil.

'On a single glass of champagne? That is not possible!' remarked Sameera.

'A single glass of champagne plus two single malts while making a very one-sided conversation with your boy toy, Gyan Singh,' said Neil.

Sameera punched him lightly in the back. 'Maybe you should dance with Gyan Singh instead of me.'

'Maybe I will,' he responded with a wink.

'It seems like you are here to woo Gyan Singh instead of me,' Sameera teased. 'You are literally so obsessed with him.'

'Woo you? Hold your horses, woman!' Neil exclaimed. 'I am here in Delhi only and only to land DJing gigs. And no other purpose.'

'Is that so, Mr Ramamurthy?' Sameera had to shout a notch higher as the DJ transitioned to a high-pitched track.

'Believe it or not, Miss Kapoor!' shouted Neil over the loud music.

'Did you miss me after I broke your heart and came back to India?' she asked him, swiftly changing the gears of this conversation.

'Gosh, I am going to regret my answer when I am sober,' replied Neil in all earnestness.

'It's okay. You can tell me,' said Sameera. 'I won't remember it anyway after the alcohol leaves my body.'

'Interesting choice of words—"after the alcohol leaves my body". You've become quite the wordsmith since you left New York City,' Neil teased her.

'Shut up and answer the question!' she quipped.

'Well . . . I did miss you. And since alcohol is making me feel brave, the truth is . . . I'm here to win you back,' said Neil shooting his shot.

'Oh, Neil!' said Sameera, breaking free from his arms and looking at him in the eye. 'It is not fair!'

'What isn't?' Neil asked, a lump in his throat.

'This. Us . . .' she said cryptically, as Neil tried to make sense of it.

'You are here all the way from the US for me. It is not fair to me because it puts me under a lot of pressure . . .' she said. 'The same happened when you proposed to me out of the blue, Neil! We had a good thing going on, but that was just too quick.'

'Sam, but . . .' Neil tried speaking but Sameera cut him short.

'This is just not fair,' Sameera repeated. 'I like you, Neil, I really do, but the timing of the whole thing is just . . .'

Neil felt a haze coming over him. He couldn't hear Sameera's voice clearly; her lips continued to move but she wasn't audible. He looked around. The DJ was still playing the music. The people were still dancing. The disco lights were still moving and flickering all over the place. He felt the club's volume fluctuate, as the atmosphere subtly shifted. Something felt off, darker. It could be his mind playing tricks on him, but he swore he could hear faint screams coming from the far end. It was probably nothing. Sameera kept talking but his mind was elsewhere.

Then it happened again. The screams pierced through the club's music. This time Sameera heard it too. She stopped speaking and stood still and alert. The DJ lowered the volume down to zero. The crowd began to murmur amongst itself. Something bad had happened but nobody knew what, when or how.

The screams became louder and the words within them became unmistakable to the naked ear.

'Fire! Fire! Fire!'

The DJ was the first one to desert his spot on the high stage and disappear into the crowd. The people right below the stage were next in line to panic and follow the DJ. Before anybody could figure it out, mass hysteria had engulfed the club.

'Neil, what is happening? Where is the fire? I don't see any fire or smoke. Why is everybody running and screaming?' Sameera cried, anxiety coating her voice.

'This doesn't make any sense. Just stick with me!' Neil assured her.

A horrific spectacle began to play out as scores of people rushed to the narrow corridor that connected the Grand Stage area to the Babylon Bar. That was where the emergency exits were.

'How can there be a fire? We had our fire safety inspection done last week! I am so confused!' Sameera told Neil.

'Sam, there might be a stampede here if we don't do anything about it!' said Neil, looking at the situation in front of his eyes.

'I have worked so hard on the opening night party. It is ruined now!' said Sameera, on the verge of tears.

'Sam, come with me. We'll talk when we are safe,' he told her, as random people pushed and shoved them aside to make it to the Emergency Exits.

'No! This cannot be happening to me . . .' said Sameera. 'I don't want to go anywhere. I'll stay right here in my club!'

'Sam, listen to me! You are having a nervous breakdown. You need to come with me to the exit. It is not safe here at all!' said Neil as a short woman wearing extra-long heels nudged past him, almost losing her balance and falling on him as she got pushed by the crowd.

'No way! I am not abandoning my club!' Sameera was adamant.

If there is one thing that he had learnt about Sameera's personality, it was that she had a steely resolve. Gosh! Where was Gyan Singh? Maybe he could put some sense into this woman! Neil stood on his toes and tried to find him. Under normal circumstances it would be easy to spot that Eiffel Tower of a human being, but no such luck right now.

As Neil scanned the hall further, his eyes came across a walkie-talkie dangling from the belt of a bouncer, who was doing a miserable job ushering people out of the situation. Neil went to the bouncer and shared an animated conversation with him, after which the bouncer uttered some words into the device. The bouncer then handed the walkie-talkie to Neil, who in turn brought it to Sameera.

'Sam, I have Gyan Singh on the line for you,' said Neil. 'Gyan Singh, this is Neil. Can you hear me? Over.'

'I hear you,' came out Gyan Singh's voice without adding 'over' at the end of his sentence. Sameera snatched the walkie from Neil's hands and spoke into it.

'Gyan Singh, what the hell is happening? Is there a fire in the club?' Her voice was angry, urgent, and desperate for a flicker of good news.

'Boss Madam, there was a small fire near the entrance of the kitchen. We controlled it before it got big. There is nothing to worry about now,' informed Gyan Singh.

'Then why are these people acting like there is a terrorist attack? It is just a small fire!' said Sameera, fuming at the situation. 'It is not even burning anymore for god's sake!'

'Sam, I have an idea. I'll try something,' Neil told her. 'We can try defusing the situation.'

Neil shoved his way through the crowd from the dance floor to the steps of the DJ's stage. He climbed up to get a vantage point of the entire situation. A sea of people tried to squeeze into the narrow corridor, which could accommodate only a handful at a time. He could finally see Gyan Singh, swimming against the tide, coming into the Grand Stage area from the corridor. All to save his precious 'Boss Madam.'

'Okay, so what do we have here?' Neil asked himself as he took stock of the things in front of him. The DJ had abandoned his very expensive controller in a bid to save his life. There was a turntable, a mixer, a microphone, a pair of gigantic headphones and a MacBook whose Apple logo had been hidden with an eggplant emoji sticker. But for Neil's plan to work, he only needed one item. He adjusted the volume and spoke directly into the mic.

'Ladies and gentlemen! Boys and Girls! Can I please have your attention?'

Except for perhaps, Sameera, Neil did not get anyone's attention. They were all busy running towards the exit and justifiably so. He made a second attempt.

'Can I please have your attention? There is no need to panic!'

He tried his best to make the crowd listen to him, but the response was the same. Sameera looked up at him from the dance floor with hopeful eyes. She prayed that the boy, whose heart she had broken, would miraculously rescue her club from this nightmare.

It was time for Neil to make a bold third attempt.

'Hello, everyone! If only I could have your kind attention for a second. I have found this Louis Vuitton bag lying on the floor. It has a bunch of gold jewelry and no ID card. Can you help me identify the owner of the bag?' asked Neil, so bold and confident as if he was 100 per cent sure that this little ploy would get people's attention. He wasn't wrong.

The words 'Louis Vuitton' and 'gold jewelry' were enough to hypnotize the people. The fleeing party-goers stopped running and turned their attention to the stage. Deep down everybody knew that the Louis Vuitton bag would be claimed by somebody else other than themselves, but the human mind can act funny and give people irrational hope.

'You, ma'am!' exclaimed Neil, pointing at the woman in the crowd with extra-long heels who had almost fallen on him a few minutes ago. 'Ma'am, did you lose your LV bag in the club tonight?'

'No, I already have my Dior bag with me,' shouted the woman to be audible in the frenzy, as she proudly raised a green saddle bag in her hands for everybody to see.

'Okay,' said Neil. 'Are you missing an LV bag, ma'am?' Neil asked another random woman from the crowd.

'It is not mine!' said the random woman dejectedly, as if she were angry at herself for letting this opportunity of a lifetime slide.

Neil saw that most people had his attention now. It was now time to go for the kill.

'Okay, everybody! I will come to the bag later. I have an important update for you. There is no fire at Kapital. It was a false alarm,' he said into the mic. 'There is no need to panic. Please don't leave. The only fire this club needs right now is on this dead dance floor!'

His joke was met with nervous laughter from the crowd. However, there was still disbelief and confusion. Fire or no fire, the mood for merrymaking had been killed.

Sameera realized that even though Neil had progressed in gaining people's attention, it would take a little more to convince them to stay at the party. She swiftly climbed the high steps of the DJ stage and joined Neil at the top.

'Friends, this is me, Sameera Kapoor!' she announced to the audience after taking the mic from Neil. 'I am really grateful that you have come to attend Kapital's opening night party! I assure you that there is no fire at the club. Everybody is safe here.'

Her words had the desired effect as the general sense of chaos and havoc eased a notch lower. The energy of the room had begun its transition to be positive.

'Please, there is no need to panic and leave the club. The Olympus bar will be serving some signature cocktails for all of you. Please relax and enjoy the night. This party ain't over!' she further appealed to everybody.

The short lady in the really long heels was the first person to start walking towards the bar. One by one many others followed suit.

Neil pressed some keys on the mixer console in front of him and dropped some funky beats on the speakers before taking the mic back from Sameera and announcing:

'Ladies and Gentlemen! The party never stops at Kapital!'

There was a loud positive cheer from a particular section of the crowd, who instantaneously scudded to the dance floor and broke into their jams.

'You did it!' Neil whispered into Sameera's ears.

'We did it!' she corrected him and kissed him on the cheek.

And then the sprinklers turned on.

6

Damp Squib

Small Fire, Big Splash

Delhi Glitz Staff
13 April 2025

One of Delhi's most iconic night clubs,
which was set to make a comeback to the party
circuit after a hiatus of five years, has had
a fire incident on 12 April, Saturday.

Delhi-ites, as we like to call ourselves,
had gotten accustomed to looking at huge
billboards that advertised the club in every
nook and corner of the city. Furthermore, it
was reported that on Friday, 11 April, every
fifth ad played on FM radio was for Kapital.
Clearly, expectations were sky-high for the

club to make a rocking comeback. But it wasn't meant to be.

One of the party-goers, who wishes to remain anonymous, stated that the opening night party at Kapital was 'absolutely fantabulous', but it had to be cut short because a fire broke down at the club. The fire was addressed quickly and as per the protocol. But there was a panic created among the people who wanted to leave the venue. After all, who can blame them for choosing prevention over cure?

Sameera Kapoor, the club's owner, took charge of the situation and ensured that everything was fine, and the party would continue. But as luck (or the lack of it) would have it, mere seconds after making a heroic statement on the stage, the water sprinklers came on due to a technical glitch in the electrical circuit. Everybody in attendance was wet (at least not in the way they had initially hoped for at the start of the party) and completely drenched in water. It all started with a fire and ended as a damp squib. Phew!

We can't help but draw comparisons between Sameera Kapoor and her mother, Maya Kapoor, who was a popular socialite and businesswoman. Maya was responsible for successfully managing both The Grand Majestic Hotel and Kapital Club after her husband, Harsh's untimely death. It will be interesting for our new readers to know that Maya Kapoor breathed her last in Kapital, five years ago, courtesy of a sudden cardiac arrest on her own birthday.

Only time will tell if Kapital is able to make a resurgence back into Delhi's nightlife. Or if Sameera Kapoor can fill her mother's heels? Keep checking back to know more.

Sameera shut the iPad and swapped it for the newspapers on the side table. At least they would be more forgiving. But the headlines were all equally piercing if not more. *'Monsoon comes early at a capital club'*, *'Opening night fiesta turns into a rain-dance party'* and *'Fire, Water and Chaos . . .'* A rival club had cheekily inserted an advertisement right next to Kapital's disaster news. *'Of course, we will serve you water, but only with your whiskey.'* She'd had enough. She tossed the newspapers into the pool. One of the papers floated for a few meters before reaching a toddler, wearing a pair of shoulder floaters. He picked the newspaper up and used it as a paddle to splash water on his mother, who was not amused by her son's antics. Neil, who was watching the entire episode, wanted to make a witty comment, but sensing Sameera's mood, he decided against it.

They were both seated on the ultra-comfortable sun loungers by the swimming pool of The Grand Majestic Hotel. Neil wore an open half-sleeve shirt, a pair of swimming trunks and a hat. Sameera was in her yoga pants and white tee with a giant avocado illustration at its centre. It was around 5 p.m., but the April sun was still burning at max capacity. Two glasses of iced Irish coffee lay on the table between the both of them.

'Tabloid journalism should be banned from the country,' said Sameera, taking a long thirsty sip from her drink.

'Why? What was in the article? Was it really bad?' asked Neil, as he watched the young mother remove scraps of the newspaper from the toddler's mouth who had evidently escalated the mess in the pool.

'It was the worst article that I have ever read in my entire life. Period!' exclaimed Sameera.

'Jeez, it sounds awful,' said Neil, as the mother called time on the toddler's stint in the pool and withdrew him from the water.

'I mean how dare they compare my Mom and me as businesswomen?' scorned Sameera. 'She had so much support, and I am all by myself. And how dare they write Kapital off? This is just not fair. Neil, are you even listening?'

The toddler and the mother were gone. Neil turned to Sameera and said, 'Of course, I am listening, Sam!

It is downright unprofessional to write sensational articles like this! Shame on them!'

'I know, right!' said Sameera, slurping her drink as a familiar figure appeared before them.

'Miss Kapoor, I have come here to apologize to you,' said Chef Alex Matthews, his head bowed.

'Chef Alex! I didn't expect you here!' said Sameera, surprised by his sudden appearance at the scene. 'Apologize for what?'

'I am sorry for spoiling the party last night,' said the chef.

'You don't have to apologize. It was an accident. Stuff like this happens, chef,' said Sameera.

'The fire accident happened near the kitchen, which is my area. I take full responsibility for negligence,' said the chef.

Neil was curious about which route Sameera would take now. Would she be the harsh taskmaster who is not afraid to throw venomous truth bombs? Or would she be the benevolent leader who rallies her troops up even after they make mistakes?

'It is not your fault, chef. Don't beat yourself up for it,' she said. 'Kapital has risen from its ashes like a phoenix. It can't afford to be bothered by small roadblocks.'

So, Sameera chose 'the benevolent leader' route after all. *Interesting choice*, thought Neil.

'Kapital is a phoenix indeed, Miss Kapoor. Thank you for your faith in me,' said the chef and left the scene after giving a slight bow.

'Your staff worships you,' said Neil as soon as Chef Alex was out of the vicinity.

'Worship, my foot. I think it is just some good ol' fashioned ass-licking,' said Sameera, giving an uncharacteristically honest opinion.

'Woah! You have become quite the judge of character,' said Neil.

'Nothing prepares you for the world like running a one-woman show!' remarked Sameera.

'Pearls of wisdom! I have a question for you, if I may,' said Neil.

'A question? Shoot, Mr Ramamurthy,' said Sameera, getting up from the sun lounger to directly face Neil.

'Okay so,' began Neil, 'as a leader, would you be rather feared or loved?'

'Hmm,' said Sameera closing her eyes and thinking deeply. 'I've never really thought about it before. But I guess that I would rather be feared more than loved as a leader.'

'And why do you say so?' he asked.

'Being loved would mean that I would have to go easy on people. And people sometimes look at that as a weakness. You know what . . .?' she asked him.

'What?'

Sameera closed her eyes for some time, and then said, 'A few months after Dad passed away, Mom came home one day fuming with anger. She told me, "Sam, for the world I am a hapless widow trying to look after my dead husband's business empire. They are not wrong. But I can never admit this else they will devour me, and everything that we have will be finished.'"

'It must have been a really difficult phase for your mother!' Neil replied.

'It was! But my mother had mastered the technique of balancing it out. She was tough as an oak at work and easy-going with me. After a few years, nobody dared to think that she was a single naïve woman in charge of such a huge business operation,' Sameera elaborated.

'Wow! Her story is downright inspiring!' said Neil.

'She was the best!' said Sameera, her tone just a notch shy of sentimental.

Sameera's phone rang. She answered it and listened to what the caller had to say. At the end of the conversation, she said, 'Okay, I am reaching there in two.'

Neil and Sameera opened the big heavy doors of Kapital and were instantly greeted by a sharp pungent smell.

'Looks like an entire truckload of floor cleaners was dumped here!' said Neil, laughing at his own little joke and tiptoeing over the freshly mopped floor.

Gyan Singh, who was waiting by the Babylon Bar, either did not hear Neil's joke or heard it and chose not to react. Gyan Singh was accompanied by a tall lanky man wearing an ill-fitted suit and reeking of cheap aftershave. He held a small briefcase in one hand and in the other a folder full of important-looking documents.

'Boss Madam, all the water has been cleared out from the floor,' informed Gyan Singh.

'What a relief!' remarked Sameera. 'Did you check the CCTVs as I asked? I want to know what caused the bloody fire.'

'The system is fried,' said Gyan Singh. 'The camera system short-circuited because of the water. The technician spent three hours trying to repair it but I am afraid all the footage has been lost.'

'Wonderful! This day couldn't get any better,' quipped Sameera. 'How much is the damage to our property?'

'Well . . .' began Gyan Singh. 'The stampede caused minor breakages to the glasses, flutes and plates.'

'Forget about the crockery, Gyan Singh. Tell me about the real deal. The alcohol and the music system?' she asked before Gyan Singh could finish debriefing her.

'The insurance agent will brief you about that,' said Gyan Singh gesturing to the tall lanky man.

'Hi, I am Puneet Saxena from NSM Insurance,' said the man, holding his hand out for Sameera to shake, to which she obliged.

'So, Mr Saxena tell me about the damage," she told him. "Hit me with all the hard numbers,'

'Ma'am, a lot of your alcohol bottles were damaged. Somewhere to the tune of thirty-five lakh. But as you know, the alcohol doesn't come under the purview of our company . . . we will not be able to cover that loss,' said Mr Saxena.

'I am aware of that. Tell me about the stuff that is within your scope?' demanded Sameera.

'Ma'am, the water from the sprinklers did a lot of damage to your electrical equipment, your speakers, disco lights, DJ console and video recording equipment. All are bust. The approximate damage is to the tune of four-and-a-half crore,' said Mr Saxena.

'Which the insurance company will pay me!' Sameera was quick to state a fact.

'I am afraid not, ma'am,' said Mr Saxena, as he ran a handkerchief over his sweating forehead.

'But the club is covered by insurance against fire!' said Neil, as he switched gears from being a passive observer to an active participant in the proceedings. 'Sameera showed me the document this morning itself!'

'You are absolutely correct, sir. The club is covered under the fire policy. But was there any fire during the time of this incident?' asked Mr Saxena.

'YES! There was a small fire near the kitchen!' said Sameera, her face red with anger. 'You *know* there was a fire! That is the entire reason that you are here standing in front of us! What kind of a question is that?'

'Yes, I agree, Miss Kapoor, and that fire was quickly extinguished according to the information that I have,' said Mr Saxena.

Nobody from Sameera, Neil or Gyan Singh replied because they knew where the conversation was headed. Mr Saxena continued anyway.

'All the damage to your expensive equipment is because of the water. Not fire.'

'But the water sprinklers turned on because of a glitch in the system!' Sameera protested, but deep down she knew the battle was already lost.

'Yes, the water sprinklers were switched on because of a technical glitch in the system. But I am sorry, the company cannot address any claim for water damage due to whatever reason as per the policy documents,' said Mr Saxena handing out a big dossier of documents to Sameera.

But Sameera didn't need to read those documents. She already knew what was in them. She had scrutinized every single word before putting her signatures on those documents.

Half an hour later, the insurance inspector was gone. The trio of Neil, Sameera and Gyan Singh sat on the adjacent bar stools.

'So, what are we going to do now, Boss Madam? Seems like the insurance is a dead end,' said Gyan Singh.

'These insurance companies are a bunch of low life scamsters!' remarked Neil.

'I will put in the money again. All of it!' said Sameera suddenly and without emotion, causing the other two to look at her in dismay.

'What? That is insane, Sam!' said Neil. 'That is a lot of money!'

'Are you sure, Boss Madam?' asked Gyan Singh.

'I've never been surer of anything in my life,' said Sameera with stoic confidence.

'Sam, but you could fight it out in the court against the insurance company!' said Neil. 'You cannot let them get away with this daylight robbery!'

'That would take years,' said Sameera, a glimmer of passion arising in her. 'I don't want to wait that long. If Kapital is not open for business soon, then it is doomed. There won't be a Kapital 3.0. Insurance or not, I will put in the money to save my club!'

'But . . .' Neil had begun something, but he was cut short by Sameera.

'This money is peanuts in the larger scheme of things,' she said.

'You know what is best for Kapital, Sam,' said Neil solemnly. 'Trust your gut on this.'

'You lead the way, Boss Madam!' chimed in Gyan Singh with a rare display of enthusiasm.

A notification buzzed on Sameera's phone, and she wasted no time checking it out. As she read the message, her face transitioned from inspired to angry to resignation within a couple of seconds.

'What is it, Boss Madam?' Gyan Singh asked.

'Kapital has lost its licence to operate,' said Sameera.

7

The Epiphany

'Sameera, please open the door! I beg of you!' said Neil as he banged his fist hard on the door of the Presidential Suite. He had been at it for a few minutes now.

There was no response from the other end until the small green blinking light on the intercom turned red, and Neil heard Sameera's voice: 'Neil, I want to be left alone right now. Please go away.'

'Sam, please talk to me once! We can reapply for the license to operate! It won't be a big deal!' he pleaded into the intercom.

Neil heard a click from the other side and the door magically opened. Sameera stood at the doorway, the mascara in her eyes a grand mess from all the crying. Neil took half a step inside the suite, but Sameera stopped him.

'Neil,' she said. 'I know you've come from a great distance to win me back, but I don't want to give you any false hopes. The only priority in my life right now is the club. I had worked a lot to get it started again, but I failed miserably on Day One.'

'Sam, but . . .' Neil attempted to pacify her, but she wasn't done speaking yet.

'Because of the unfavorable media coverage, getting the license back will be impossible . . . Kapital was both my parents' brainchild. And with both of them dead and gone, it seemed like the best thing to do in their memory. But as it turns out, I am not capable. I am just any other rich kid who inherited her parent's millions and has no business skills of her own.'

'But Sam, I am here for you . . .' said Neil but he was cut short by Sameera again.

'Neil, I don't need anybody right now. Please Neil, leave me alone. I don't want you at this hotel and in my life right now,' she said, shutting the door on his face.

Sameera sunk into her chair and opened the small cabinet hidden at the foot of the office table in the Presidential Suite. She had to crouch a little to be able to view the full extent of her liquor stash. A tall tequila bottle with a sombrero for a cap was the first to catch her eye. *Pass!* Tequila was her happy drink. She wanted something

to drown her sorrows in. Next in line were two bottles
of red wine, both about three-quarters full. *Pass!* She
wanted something more potent. When her eyes fell
on the half-a-bottle of vodka that she had picked on
a layover in Moscow, she knew this was it. She picked
it up and immediately took a lonnnnng sip. Yes, this is
what she wanted—the alcohol igniting her throat with
acidic ferocity. She felt the burn travel all the way from
her food pipe to the stomach. With a few more sips, she
gulped the entire bottle down. Her nerves had begun to
lose sensation just as she had intended. Aah! She had
been chasing this numbness all along.

Neil found himself smoking a cigarette on the bench
outside the hotel lobby. His luggage was packed and
placed on a trolley at the far end of the entrance.

'Got a light?' asked a voice from behind.

Neil turned around to find a woman in gym gear,
holding an unlit cigarette in her hand. She looked
familiar; he couldn't place her yet.

'Yes, sure,' said Neil, bringing out his lighter.

'It was a great attempt on your part to rescue the
party last night. Hard luck that the sprinklers ruined it
ultimately,' she told him after taking her first drag and
seating herself next to him.

'Were you at the party too? I am sorry it turned out
to be such a bummer,' Neil told her.

'Oh, I was at the party all right. Too bad I couldn't claim that LV bag of yours!' she added with a chuckle.

And that is when Neil realized why she did look familiar. It was the same woman who he had singled out for the Louis Vuitton bag!

'Ha ha! Tough luck,' he said as an Uber pulled up in front of him on the porch. 'I am sorry, but I'll have to take your leave now. My ride is here.'

'Where are you headed?' she asked, slightly disappointed at the premature shutdown of the banter.

'I don't know, but somewhere far from here. My girlfriend, umm ex-girlfriend, who owns this hotel and the club, just gave me the marching orders,' Neil admitted.

'Oh, Sameera Kapoor?' she asked. 'The Sameera Kapoor? You dated the Sameera Kapoor?'

Neil nodded. 'Do you know her?'

'Only by reputation,' she said. 'Her mother was a legend- the way she rose from the ashes of a family tragedy to build this empire. Takes balls.'

'So I have heard,' said Neil.

'But the breakup must hurt,' said the woman, ashing her cigarette on the ground. 'The both of you were so pally on the stage before the sprinklers came on!'

'The bloody sprinklers are precisely why she wants me to leave! Long story short, the club burnt a lot of money due to the water damage, and lost its licence to operate,' Neil told her, throwing the fag end of his cigarette on the floor and stubbing it under his shoe.

'Oh my god, that sucks!' said the woman. 'I was so excited about Kapital!'

'That makes the two of us,' said Neil, standing up from the bench.

'Now, she wants some time off because she thinks that she has failed her dead parents. Phew!'

'What is your plan now?' asked the woman.

'I am going to check into another hotel. I have a few DJ gigs lined up at other clubs in the city,' he told her.

'No, I mean what is your plan with regards to your girlfriend and this club of hers?'

'I honestly have no idea. I am going to give this situation a few days to cool down. Maybe then I can try talking to her again. I don't know,' Neil admitted, giving his Uber driver a hand signal to indicate that he was going to be there in two minutes.

'Or maybe, you can take charge of the situation right now and win her back,' she said as she threw her finished cigarette on the floor and quashed it under her Yeezys.

'And how do you propose I do that?' asked Neil.

The Grand Majestic Hotel had three conference rooms in its armoury. Conference Room A was situated on the ground floor. It had access from the corridor across the main reception. In terms of seating capacity, it was by far the largest among the three. It was also Sameera's favourite. She used it for most of her board meetings, especially when there was a foreign delegation involved. It was also the room that her father had nicknamed 'The War Room'. A lot of important business strategies had been formulated there over the years. Sameera's mother had hinted that she had been conceived there but now there was no way of knowing for sure.

It was 9:30 p.m. Sameera entered The War Room and was surprised to see the motley group of individuals sitting at the table. Gyan Singh and Neil were the only faces that were instantly recognizable.

'Before you say anything, I want to make a few things clear,' said Neil, giving Sameera no chance to process what was going on.

'What?' asked Sameera, irritable but managing to keep her cool in front of these strangers.

'Number one, yes Gyan Singh texted you to come here on my insistence. And number two—yes, I had checked out of The Grand Majestic Hotel and was on my way out, when I had an epiphany,' said Neil.

'And what was that epiphany?' asked Sameera, settling down into the empty boss' chair at the long end of the table.

'There is a way to get Kapital out of the impossible situation it is in right now,' said Neil.

'Pray tell!' said Sameera, not able to mask her sarcasm.

'This is Mr Sahni, a legal expert in matters pertaining to restaurants, bars and clubs,' said Neil pointing towards a middle-aged man wearing round platinum earrings in his ears.

Mr Sahni gave a half bow to Sameera and said, 'Mr Neil Ramamurthy has explained the full case to me, ma'am. The decision of the local government body to revoke your club's license is without any solid grounds. I will have it reversed in a matter of days.'

'But what about their reasoning that we did not adhere to fire safety and general security guidelines?' asked Sameera, sarcasm giving way to sincerity.

'Don't worry, ma'am,' said Mr Sahni. 'If the worst comes to worst, I know just the right people in the office machinery. I'll throw in a couple of Gandhis under the table. That will clear their doubts.'

A few smirks were exchanged among everybody present in the room. Sameera seemed a bit relaxed now, hopeful too. Small victory for Neil.

'All right,' said Sameera after thinking deeply. 'I will also get you in touch with Mr Hiranandani. He is our corporate lawyer on retainer. He shall provide you with whatever resources that you might require.'

'Ah, Mr Hiranandani!' said Mr Sahni. 'I have had the pleasure of working with him on a previous matter. I am looking forward to collaborating again.'

'Perfect!' said Sameera, not getting her hopes up just yet.

'Next up, is Mr Ali,' said Neil after Mr Sahni had sat down. 'He is a sound engineer from Dubai. I was first introduced to him in New York City when he had come to install a new system for the club that I was DJing at.'

Mr Ali, a muscular man who seemed like he spent a lot of time and money on grooming his beard, offered his hand for Sameera to shake from across the table, which she did.

'I had almost boarded my flight back home when I received Neil's call,' told Mr Ali to everybody present. 'I had been in Delhi for a week to install a really sick music system at Club Paradiso.'

Sameera shrugged at the mention of her rival club. Mr Ali continued.

'I heard that rain messed up your system! But don't you worry. I am going to replace the entire thing and install the sickest system that Delhi has ever seen. Even sicker than Club Paradiso.'

'It was more like artificial rain, Mr Ali,' said Neil, pointing to the water sprinklers on the ceiling of The War Room, and the both of them shared a muted laugh.

Sameera intently listened as Neil introduced two more people who would take charge of the lighting system and on-ground security management respectively. When the last of the four was done talking, the door opened and in walked a woman wearing an Adidas Originals tracksuit and holding a Hello Kitty case in her hand. All the male heads turned towards her, mesmerized. Sameera had a feeling that she had seen her somewhere but couldn't place her exactly.

'Am I late?' the woman asked looking at Neil.

'Ladies and gentlemen, this is Pari Chadha, the last piece of the puzzle for Project Kapital 3.0, and she is also the main driving force behind the epiphany,' said Neil, winking at Pari.

'Hi everyone! It is lovely to meet you! And hello again, Sameera ma'am. We met last night at the opening party!' said Pari.

Now, Sameera was able to place her perfectly well.

'Of course, I remember you, Pari! How are you doing?' asked Sameera.

'Very well, ma'am! The party last night was fantastic; a bit unfortunate with the chaos towards the end. But a great party nevertheless,' said Pari.

'Thank you!' said Sameera earnestly. "Please call me Sameera."

'So, credit where credit is due. It was Pari who inspired me to rally the troops here in this conference room. And as it turns out, she herself also wants to become a part of this team!' said Neil.

'How wonderful!' remarked Sameera. 'We would love to have you, Pari. What can you do for us?'

'Ma'am, I mean Sameera, I figured that the club would need the services of a marketing agency on a full-time basis to reverse the debacle of last night and restore Kapital's good name,' said Pari as every eyeball in the conference room focused on her.

'My agency, A to Z Marketing Solutions, is among the top-ranked marketing agencies in the city. I am also a successful social media influencer with a following of 1.5 million on Instagram alone. Additionally, I have a team of influencers, strategists and statisticians for every marketing solution out there!'

'Wow! Welcome on board, Pari!' said Sameera. 'We'd be delighted to have you on the team!'

'Thank you,' said Pari, as she removed her rose gold MacBook from its Hello Kitty cover. 'I have made a list of pointers that I would like to share with everyone. I believe we can immediately start working on these without wasting any time,' said Pari while opening her computer screen.

'Absolutely! I would love to hear your ideas! But there is one more important thing that needs to be addressed,' said Sameera as everybody looked up at her.

'I was just informed today that Kapital's current resident DJ has jumped ship and gone to work for a rival club. So, I guess that the spot of resident DJ is up for grabs for Mr Ramamurthy, if he is interested,' said Sameera, smiling directly at Neil.

'Absolutely ma'am,' he said, breathing a huge sigh of relief. 'It would be the greatest honour of my life! Only one slight complication though.'

'What is it?' asked Sameera.

'My work visa is currently sponsored by Kapital's rivals in Delhi . . .'

'Don't worry about it, we'll take care of everything,' jumped in Sameera before he could finish speaking.

Neil smiled through the rest of the meeting. There were good signs all around. The team looked like it could accomplish this challenge. He could sense a friendship brewing between Sameera and Pari. Project Kapital 3.0 was up and running. And with it, Project-Win-Sameera-Back was also up and running.

8

Helter-Skelter

Dear Diary,

Apparently, Google is the eighth wonder of the twenty-first century. The other day, I typed in my symptoms, and voila! I received an answer within milliseconds. MILLISECONDS! Can you imagine? I wish we had such technology when I was a little boy growing up in a small fishing village in Goa, in the late 1970s. We had a know-it-all quack called Peter who served as the village doctor. You have a headache? Go to Peter. Twisted an ankle? Go to Peter. There's blood in your urine today? Go to Peter. You get the idea. And to his credit, Peter never returned an unhappy patient. Whatever his methods were, they always seemed to work! But I highly doubt that Peter would even be equipped to handle modern-day invisible problems such as anxiety, depression or the thing that Google thinks I am going through: a psychotic episode. Bleh!

Should the words 'psychotic episode' scare the lightbulbs out of my head? Google says no. It can be managed with professional guidance: T-H-E-R-A-P-Y. How will that even help me? Will a shrink magically erase the grand majestic tragedy that my life is? I doubt so. To get a better grip on reality, Google has advised me to talk or write in detail about my emotions and any possible incidents or triggers. Maintain a diary, so to speak. Okay, I'll give this a try—pouring my thoughts and memories and emotions and whatnot into this notebook. I wonder if Peter ever asked his patients to talk about their emotions. He would have to shut the shutters down of his shady little practice for sure. Anyway!

I am pretty much bummed about the whole 'fire incident' at the opening party of Kapital. In hindsight, I should have behaved better than I did. Whenever I feel agitated, my head just blanks out from reality. And when I *wake up* in the real world minutes later, I realize that I have done something extreme and beyond repair. And this is exactly what happened that night.

I saw Sameera dancing with that American skid mark of hers in front of the DJ stage. Their arms were wrapped around each other; their eyes were locked

into each other's gaze and their lips barely inches apart
from touching. I have seen Sameera when she is out
on dates with boys, and sometimes she brings them
back with her to spend the night in the Presidential
Suite. Those boys do not make me jealous. I know that
those are just flings for her. But this American boy is
different. The chemistry that he shared with Sameera
was electric. I have never seen Sameera so enamoured
with somebody like this ever before. These bloody
Americans are always trying to interfere in the affairs
of the rest of the world!

When I could not digest seeing the American dirty
dancing with my girl anymore, I blanked out and went
into one of my psychotic episodes.

When I came to my senses, the chaos had already
begun. I was confused. Why were the people running
helter-skelter everywhere in the club? Then I saw it.
There was a fire near where I was standing. Not an
enormous one, but something decently big to make
these rich bastards shit their pants. As much as
I liked the fire disrupting the party, I had to act as
if I were a responsible and rational member of the
hotel's staff (and society in general). I went inside the
kitchen and barked at my team to quickly fetch the fire
extinguishers, and ultimately led the effort to kill the
fire, which may or may not have been started by me.

A few minutes later, I heard Neil's voice on the
speakers. He was urging the party-goers to not abandon
the party. Bloody fool. What did he think? That people

would listen to him blabbering in his foolish American accent? This is Delhi. Not the United States. People here are sheep. They blindly follow the crowd. And the crowd was headed towards the exit.

But then the strangest thing happened. I saw the people actually calming down a bit. Some people had already left the party, but the remaining majority had begun to see sense in that American killjoy's words. I had a vision of Sameera dancing even more closely with him after his heroic feat of saving the party. And in all certainty, they would exchange some bodily fluids by the end of the night. I could not let that happen. Not on my watch. I wish he had choked on the shrimp cocktail and died.

I recalled the day when the sprinkler system was being installed. The company technician was briefing Sameera and her team about the manual button that could switch the sprinklers on in case the automatic sensors failed. I retrieved that little nugget of memory from my brain to cause rain in the club. Mission finally accomplished. No more dirty dancing for the night. Everybody goes home and sleeps in their own beds.

I don't know if these so-called psychotic episodes are such a bad thing after all. Maybe Peter would have asked me to just sleep it off and feel better in the morning. But I will never know for sure. It is a bit unfortunate that Peter got his head smashed by my father, who caught him with my mother after too many visits about her recurring migraine.

There will come a day when Sameera appreciates all that I have done for her. I can go to any lengths for her. After all, she is turning out to be a spitting image of her mother, Maya.

9

The Economics of Kitty Parties

The look that Neil had chosen to go for today, after half an hour of dress changes, was simple and chic. He wore a cream linen shirt over white trousers paired with his green Nike Air Jordans. A metallic link chain rested against his chest, an overkill but often the unofficial uniform of professional DJs.

It was still early days following Kapital's re-relaunch after the fire sprinkler disaster. The crowd did return but the numbers were still far from satisfactory or profit-making. The guest DJs with whom the club had signed contracts before had either declined to come back or charged an obscene amount of money because the job came with a 'significant risk to life'. So, Neil was the only DJ who played for the initial few days. He did not mind that in the least for two reasons:

A. His food and lodging were taken care of by The Grand Majestic Hotel.

B. He got to spend more time around Sameera, who had softened up more during the execution of Project Kapital 3.0.

It was 2 p.m. in the afternoon, and Neil tried to amp the party up with his most trusted tracks that always got the audience grooving. But today the crowd in front of him seemed largely unimpressed. It was a group of eighteen ladies in their early to mid-forties, attending their kitty party at Kapital. They sipped on cocktails and chatted amongst themselves while an abandoned game of Tambola, blingy designer bags and sunglasses lay on a large table (which actually was a combination of four small tables joined together) in front of them. Neil, who had been playing for quite some time now, finally put on a random playlist of 'All Time Bollywood Hit Songs' from YouTube, which made the ladies come to the dance floor. Once satisfied that the party had caught steam, Neil came down to have a drink at the bar. Sameera was already sitting by herself, sipping on an ice-cold orange juice from a straw.

'A whiskey on the rocks, please!' he told the barkeep as he took the seat next to Sameera.

'Daytime drinking, eh?' teased Sameera.

'Yes ma'am. It is an occupational hazard,' he replied.

'I've been here for half an hour. I see that you are quite a hit with the crowd!' she said, teasing him more.

'Oh, give me a break! None of my songs seemed to be working for these women!' he ranted to her. 'Ultimately, I had to put a Bollywood number to get them to move their booties!'

'Tough crowd you've got. But trust me, they care more about the DJ than his songs,' said Sameera.

'What do you mean?' said Neil trying hard to control himself from blushing after this unexpected piece of information.

'Well, look at them! They could be happily sitting at their table and playing Teen Patti or Tambola or whatever it is that they like to indulge in. But here they are on the dance floor trying to impress the DJ,' Sameera told him.

'But they just came to the dance floor some time ago . . .' reasoned Neil.

'That is true Mr DJ, but what you couldn't notice from that stage of yours is that they've been eyeing you ever since the party began!' said Sameera nonchalantly.

The barkeep placed Neil's drink in front of him, and Neil took a long sip so that he could buy some time before replying to Sameera.

'You are kidding, right?' he finally asked.

'I am serious. It is just harmless ogling from their side, though. You shouldn't be scared that they'll make a pass or anything at you. Unless you are into that kind of thing,' said Sameera, and broke into a peal of laughter.

'I am not into that kind of thing. Thank you for your concern,' said Neil, a little embarrassed.

'No judgement here buddy,' said Sameera shrugging both her hands in the air. 'Relax, I am just pulling your leg. But love them or hate them, these kitty parties are a necessary requirement for restaurants and clubs like ours to function during the day.'

'Elaborate,' demanded Neil, a little intrigued.

'Okay, so first of all, you are familiar with the entire concept of kitty parties, right?' asked Sameera.

'Nope! Heard it for the first time when this booking came in two days ago,' admitted Neil.

'All right then, a kitty party is a woman-only social gathering,' began Sameera.

'That bit is very evident,' said Neil, looking at the dance floor where a group of the ladies had created a sub-group and was now vigorously performing the hook step of a Bollywood number.

'Most of these women, I'd say at least 90 per cent, are stay-at-home wives. They plan their monthly outings with the other stay-at-home wives in their social circles. These social gatherings happen either over brunch or in the afternoon. The women negotiate a per-head rate with the club or restaurant which includes food and beverages,' said Sameera.

'That sounds fun! I wish I could do it with my boys too!' said Neil, swirling his glass in his hand, hoping that the ice would melt a little faster and his whiskey would get a tad bit more diluted.

'Most clubs and restaurants offer special kitty party packages during the day because business is anyway slow during those hours,' said Sameera.

'So, this is an Indian version of Happy Hours but exclusively for women?' asked Neil.

'Exactly,' said Sameera.

'It seems like a win-win for these women and the clubs!' said Neil.

'Exactly.'

Neil finished the remainder of his drink in one big slurp. He then got off his bar stool and proceeded to walk towards the stage.

'Where are you going all of a sudden?' Sameera called behind him.

'These women who are hosting their kitty party are very important clients of the club. It would be rude if the DJ went missing for such a long time!' said Neil, which made Sameera laugh.

'Go get them, tiger!' she cheered after him as he took his place on the stage. The women from the kitty party gave him a loud cheer and in return for their energy, Neil played a catchy Hindi number, which immediately pumped the women.

Neil opened the notes folder on his phone and made the following entry:

Need to learn more Hindi songs

10

Circadian Rhythm

'How is it going, my long-lost friend? I haven't seen you forever!' Emily asked through the iPad screen which lay on the centre table in the living room of the Presidential Suite.

'It is going well! The clients are happy,' Sameera told from across the sofa where she sat cross-legged in plain black pajamas and a Garfield T-shirt. 'We should be able to break even soon! The numbers look encouraging!'

'You know that I am not asking about the club!' Emily pestered at her best friend. Sameera blushed a deep shade of red.

'It is going fine with Neil. He has been instrumental in getting the club up and running again,' said Sameera.

'Can we keep Kapital aside for a bit?' asked Emily. 'Tell me how it is going between both of you! God, why are you being so difficult to talk to? Come on spill the beans, girl!'

'There are no beans to spill. Neil is in Delhi and is going to be here for some time since Kapital has hired him as the Resident DJ. He is happy with the arrangement so far!'

'Oh, you naughty girl!' said Emily, excited at hearing this bit of information. 'You couldn't bring yourself to make a pass directly at him! So, you hired him as the DJ for your club. Nice! I like where this is going!'

'*This* is not going anywhere! Our relationship is strictly professional and nothing else,' said Sameera, trying to be as emphatic as possible, an effort she knew was in vain.

'Professional my ass. I am happy that you have made progress with your star-crossed lover,' Emily said, her wicked sense of humour awakened.

'He is not my star-crossed lover! Em, can you please not?' said Sameera, half-annoyed and half-amused.

'Okay fine, Sam, take a chill pill, will you?' said Emily, steering the course of the conversation in another direction. 'Tell me about the club! How has it picked up since *the night* that you've banned me from talking about?'

Sameera breathed a sigh of relief. She would rather talk about her professional than personal life.

'The club has actually managed to pick up a bit since we opened it again. The numbers aren't as strong as we projected in its initial run, but we are making slow but steady progress. Can't complain,' said Sameera, making a 'V' for 'victory' with two fingers.

'And this slow-but-steady progress is the courtesy of Mr American DJ?' quipped Emily.

'Oh my god! I can't believe you're back at it!' Sameera blushed. 'But you're right. I asked him to leave me alone after the club license was revoked. He almost left but came back with a plan to get the club restarted. Sometimes it feels like he is more driven to get the club back on track than I am!'

'Maybe he has figured out that the way to your heart is through Kapital after all!' said Emily giving a sincere smile.

Sameera smiled back and didn't say anything, because in her heart she knew that Emily was right.

Neil loved Tuesdays. Tuesdays meant that there wasn't any DJ duty. And he could hop into his bed on time, like a normal functioning adult. He had seen a YouTube video once where it was preached that to optimize one's life, one has to strictly adhere to the body's circadian rhythm, which basically meant waking up early with the sunrise and going to sleep early as soon as it got dark. As a professional DJ, Neil had been showing the middle finger to his body's circadian rhythm on six out of seven days of the week. But on Tuesdays, he pretended to be a regular man with a regular job, where he didn't have a duty to attend to individuals who were drunk out of their brains. Tonight, he went to bed at 9 p.m. after an early dinner. His phone dinged as soon as he switched the lights off and slipped inside the covers. He resisted the temptation to check his phone for five seconds before he finally gave in.

(Maa) Did she say yes?
(Neil) Maa, stop asking me the same question over and over!
(Maa) Okay, no need to get angry. I am your mother. I have a right to ask

Neil took a long deep breath before he replied again.

(Neil) I miss you, Maa!
(Maa) I miss you too, my kiddo <3
(Neil) Come to India, please! I want to be with you! It has been almost two months since I last saw you!
(Maa) Soon kiddo! But you know how things are right? The school vacations don't start for another month. I can't abandon these kids just before their examinations
(Neil) :(
(Maa) :*
(Neil) o:)
(Maa) You should catch up on your sleep. It is Tuesday

(Neil) Yes, Maa
(Maa) Goodnight!
(Neil) Goodnight!

Alex Matthews's Diary Entry, 17 May 2025

Dear Diary,

I think I have gotten used to spilling my thoughts into you. Google was right. This exercise indeed calms me down. I have somebody to talk to. Somebody who would understand me without an iota of judgement. To normal people, it would appear to be acts of insanity and unhealthy obsession. But to you, Dear Diary, everything is as it is. Black and white. No scope for grey.

Today I want to write about the day my life changed forever. If this day had not taken place, I would probably never have become *the* Alex Matthews. None of the celebrity chef-TV show judge-magazine coverage mumbo-jumbo. I would be just Alex. A nobody lost in the crowd of millions. It was destiny that I met her that day.

I was in my late teens when I first saw her. She stepped out of a red Mercedes-Benz car, dressed in a green skirt and a stylish black top. Her face was covered by a pair of large glasses. A chauffeur rushed behind her with an open umbrella to protect her delicate skin from the harmful rays of the sun. She was a Goddess walking into Connaught Place, a market where we mere mortals worked to earn our livelihood.

I was behind the register when she came inside the restaurant and took a corner table for two. Her chauffeur stayed outside to keep vigil, like a loyal watchdog. My Uncle Martin, who owned the restaurant, asked me to go take her order since we were short-staffed that day. Nervous energy engulfed the entirety of my body. I had never spoken to such a beautiful woman ever even in my dreams.

'Ma'am, order please?' I asked her, a notepad and pen in my trembling hands.

'One cappuccino, please,' she told me in her beautiful angelic voice.

The year was somewhere in the mid 90's and the concept of cappuccino, the foreign-style coffee, had just become the rage in the market. My Uncle Martin was a pioneer of the cappuccino movement in Delhi. He had imported a cappuccino-making machine from Italy for his restaurant and had heavily advertised it all across Delhi. It wasn't uncommon for people to come to Martin's Corner just to sip the new trendy beverage.

'One cappuccino . . .' I repeated the order as I wrote it down on my pad, except that the pen wouldn't work. Stupid pen. I tried to give it a little shake, but it still did not work. She saw my dilemma and almost laughed. She took the pen from my hands and removed its cap. In my nervousness, I had forgotten to uncap it! This

was the most embarrassed that I had ever been in
my life. I wanted the earth to open up and swallow me
whole. I swear!

'What is your name?' she asked me as she handed
the wretched pen back to me.

'Alex,' I replied, avoiding eye contact from the
humiliation.

'Are you new here? I have never seen you before!'

'He is my nephew, ma'am,' said my Uncle Martin,
magically appearing from thin air into the scene. 'I have
asked him to help out at the restaurant during his
summer break.'

'Such a hard-working boy,' she said, looking at me.
'During my summer vacations, I would just lie by the
swimming pool!'

'Don't encourage him, ma'am!' Uncle Martin cut her
in between. 'This lad likes to waste time anyway. He is
always in the kitchen attempting dishes from cuisines
that nobody's ever heard of!'

My head was still hung down in shame.

'Oh, Martin! Don't be a buzzkill. He loves cooking! This
is brilliant! He can be a great asset to your restaurant!'
said the lady, giving sound advice to my Uncle Martin,
who had an immense God-given gift to ignore logic.

'I already have two chefs at the restaurant, ma'am,'
said Uncle Martin as he whacked my head with just
enough force that I would not shriek out loud. 'I need
somebody to look after the register. That is where real
business skills are used. Cooking requires no skills!'

'May I join in the conversation, if you guys don't mind?'

The three of us looked up to see a handsome man in dark bootcut jeans, a white shirt and a brown leather jacket standing behind us. The lady immediately stood up and gave him a peck on the lips. Uncle Martin's posture stiffened up a bit as he recognized the person.

'Mr Harsh Kapoor! Please come and sit! You are here after a long time!' said my uncle.

'Yes, long time indeed, Martin. I was in Paris for two months scouting for a new hotel chain to invest in. I wanted to stay longer, but my ladylove here,' he said, putting his arm around the prettiest woman that I had seen in my life. 'She sent her strict orders that she wants me back in Delhi. So, here I am!'

'How lovely to have you, sir! What will you have?' asked Uncle Martin.

'I will have a black coffee as usual. And my lady will have a cappuccino, as usual.'

'I was just placing the order for the cappuccino when you arrived!' said the lady.

'Maya, it is time to accept that I can read every little thought in your brain!' he teased her.

'Very funny!' said the lady, whose name was Maya, I just learned.

'We will excuse you both,' said Uncle Martin. 'Get their coffees!' he said turning towards me.

'Who is this young fellow? I have never seen him before?' asked Mr Kapoor.

Maya answered before I or Uncle Martin could speak.

'He is Alex. Martin's nephew. He's really passionate about cooking!'

'That's great! Maybe we could give him a job at The Grand Majestic as a chef in a few years,' Mr Kapoor said.

Later that night, when I was in bed, I achieved clarity on two ambitions for my life:

1. I wanted to be a chef and get a job at Mr Harsh Kapoor's hotel.
2. I was in love with Maya, and I would do anything to be with her.

11

Single Tick

Neil was running late for the meeting. The rest of the think-tank, comprising Sameera and Pari, was already at Kapital, waiting for him. He pressed the button for the elevator and waited till it arrived. When it finally did after what seemed like hours, he scudded inside, pressing the button for the twentieth floor. The elevator cruised past the floors. 1, 2, 3 . . . 10. As it reached the eleventh floor, it stopped abruptly with a jolt and threw a misbalanced Neil down on the floor.

'Shucks!' he screeched as loud as he could, getting up from the floor and standing upright on his two feet.

The lights began flickering and so did the little digital board which displayed the floor number. Neil anxiously pressed the 'Open Doors' button but nothing happened. There was an emergency button next to a small microphone and a speaker. Neil buried his finger into that button and spoke into the microphone.

'Hello! Is anybody there? I am stuck in the elevator in Tower A of the hotel!'

No response came back.

'Hello, this is Neil Ramamurthy. I'm stuck in the elevator! Please get me out of here!'

No response.

Neil brought his phone out to call Sameera, but as luck would have it, there was no reception.

'Damn it!' he cursed at the top of his lungs. He moved his phone all around the box that he was trapped in to maybe catch the faintest bit of network reception possible. No result.

Claustrophobia kicked in and Neil began sweating. Trickle by trickle at first, and then profusely. He banged at the door and yelled for help. He pressed all the buttons at random to achieve something, anything at all. Nothing happened. He shouted. Jumped. Punched. Kicked. Nothing. He felt his head spin. And then the lights went out.

'Once a week jazz nights are going to do wonders for the club! Mark my words!' Pari told Sameera.

'I love jazz more than anybody, but I am not sure if it is a good direction for the club!' Sameera admitted.

They were both seated at a table by a big glass window in Kapital. It made for a breathtaking panoramic view of the city from up there. Pari wore a navy Ralph Lauren Polo Bear top with jeans and high ankle boots, while Sameera was in her grey Versace sailor pants, an Armani denim top and flat shoes. Business outfits for both of them.

'If I had to give you only one advice and one advice only, I would say that please, please give jazz a serious thought!' said Pari. 'Kapital could host fabulous jazz nights once a week!'

'Okay, if you insist. We could give it a try!' said Sameera. 'By the way, where is Neil? He was supposed to be here by now!'

'I have no idea! He texted on the WhatsApp group some fifteen minutes ago that he was on his way up here!' said Pari, simultaneously opening the Kapital Think Tank group chat on her phone.

'Where are you? @NeilRamamurthy,' Pari texted on the group. WhatsApp only showed a single tick against his name.

'I'll try calling him!' said Sameera and dialled his number. 'Unreachable.'

'Okay, he will probably join us in a bit,' said Pari, after the both of them had reached a dead end in their efforts. 'Let me tell you about some of the other ideas that I have for the club!'

'Sure,' said Sameera as a waiter placed a bowl of soup each in front of them.

'So, this is going to sound a bit outlandish but just hear me out,' said Pari before blowing over the piping hot soup in her spoon.

'Don't worry!' said Sameera, sipping the soup. 'Who knows? We might strike gold!'

'How about a silent disco night?' said Pari excitedly.

'Elaborate, please. I am not familiar with the concept.'

'Okay so, a silent disco is a Western concept, forced into existence by sound pollution activists. You wear wireless headphones on the dance floor, and the DJ directly plays the music into your headphones. There is no sound on the speakers. To a person who is not wearing headphones, it is as if he's walked into a school library. Pin-drop silence.'

'Hard pass,' said Sameera, giving a thumbs down. 'These concepts might work in London or New York. But this is Delhi. The success of the party is judged by how loud it is!'

'Fair point,' said Pari, a bit dejected. 'The next idea is that of a glow-in-the-dark party.'

'What is a glow-in-the-dark party?' asked Sameera, feeling bad for being unenthusiastic about both of Pari's ideas so far. She needed Neil to share some of her burden. Gosh! Where was he?

'The club will be made as dark as possible by shutting almost all lights,' Pari began narrating her third idea for the day, but she was cut short by Sameera.

'But babe, we can't shut all lights. We have to keep the bar lights on and of course, all the lights that mark the exits. We can't take a chance after that opening night fiasco.'

'Of course,' said Pari, annoyed at being interrupted but still choosing to carry on. 'Anyway, the club will be as dark as possible. All essential lighting will not be compromised. The attendees will be given glow-in-the-dark paints to put on their bodies and clothes. We can even hand out glow sticks as props.'

'And we play music as usual!' Sameera chimed in. 'None of that silent disco nonsense. This actually might work out. It's a great idea!' said Sameera, much to Pari's relief.

'I'll ask my team to work the costs out,' said an elated Pari.

'Awesome!' said Sameera, as she took her phone out and wrote a WhatsApp message to Neil on a private window:

Where the hell are you?

Only a single tick graced the bottom of the text. Frustrated, Sameera returned to her conversation with Pari.

'Pari, by the way, where are we with the promotions of the Spin Twins?'

'Oh, they are going on great,' said Pari, still struggling with the hot soup. 'This is the Spin Twins' first show in India. You are very lucky to have landed them for Kapital.'

'Neil gets the credit on this one,' said Sameera beaming with joy. 'We managed to sign them through his connections. The Spin Twins are among the Top 100 DJs in the world right now! I can't wait to see the madness they stir at Kapital!'

'How are you ladies liking the soup?'

Both the women looked up to see Chef Alex standing next to their table.

'The soup is great!' said Pari, who had barely tasted it so far.

'It tastes a little different today, but I like it nevertheless,' said Sameera.

'You have a sharp sense of taste, boss, just like your mother,' said Chef Alex.

'The slight difference in taste is because of cloves! I noticed that you had a slightly sore throat when you placed the order. Now wait for the cloves to do their thing.'

'How thoughtful, chef. Thank you!' said Sameera, taking a sip of the soup to truly express her gratitude.

'The cloves are a great touch. I am loving the soup,' said Pari.

'Thank you,' said Chef Alex, taking a half bow.

'Oh shit,' said Sameera as she suddenly stood up from her chair with a jump, making both Chef Alex and Pari perplexed. A sweating Neil, the colour drained from his face, reached their table along with Gyan Singh in tow.

'Neil, are you all right?' asked Sameera, making him sit in her chair. 'Where were you? What happened? We were so worried!'

'The ele . . . elevator!' said Neil with great difficulty.

'Here, have some water!' said Chef Alex, handing Neil a glass which he gulped down instantly. Remarkable recovery reflected on Neil's face after a few seconds. The stutter was gone, and the anxiety eased a few notches down.

'The elevator stopped working midway. I was trapped with no network reception and no light,' he told them.

'Did you try the emergency button?' asked Pari.

'I did, but there was no response! None of the buttons seemed to work.'

'Good heavens!' said Sameera with sympathy. 'How did you get out then?'

'It magically started working on its own,' said Neil. 'When the doors finally opened, there was Gyan Singh standing along with a technician.'

'There was a minor short circuit in the electricals, Boss Madam,' Gyan Singh chipped in. 'As soon as the hotel staff got to know about it, it was fixed.'

'Thank God,' said Sameera. 'I'll get to the bottom of this. This shouldn't be happening with our lifts. I cannot afford another disaster for God's sake!'

'It is okay, actually. If it were not for my claustrophobia, I may have survived this gracefully. Thankfully the elevators don't have cameras,' said

Neil, trying to diffuse the situation with a little bit of humour, now that he felt much better.

'Neil, you sit and relax for a bit. Chef Alex has made this excellent soup that you must try!' said Sameera, passing her bowl to him.

12

Party Animal

In his few days as the Resident DJ for Kapital, Neil had gone through a spectrum of experiences. There were good times—when the club was flooded with people, and they were receptive to his brand of techno and house music. Those were the days when he felt fulfilled as an artist and creator of music, and not just a mere DJ who blindly played pre-recorded music.

Then there were the okayish times—when the crowd was just there and not necessarily responding to his music but having a good time on their own. Neil honestly did not mind those times. And then there were the bad experiences- when somebody would walk up to him on the stage and slip him a chit of paper with a Punjabi song title written on it. He had put himself under an enormous burden already by learning

Bollywood music. Punjabi was an altogether different ball game. *Phew!*

'Why do these people think that I know Punjabi songs just because I look Indian?' he would often complain to Sameera. 'I have Tamilian roots, Jeez! I won't be half as offended if I got requests for Tamilian songs!'

'Sorry to burst your bubble, but nobody is going to put in a request for any Tamilian songs,' Sameera told him as they stood on the balcony of the twentieth floor. 'Just give them what they want, Neil. It's bad enough that after the fire incident, people are still reluctant to party here. The numbers sure are picking up, but till the time we don't successfully have the Spin Twins' night, we will have to keep our heads low and toe the line.'

'But Sam, Punjabi songs!' Neil protested.

'You're already working on your Hindi music. Think of Punjabi music as the same as Hindi but on steroids. It is good for business,' said Sameera, smiling at her own justification.

'Sometimes I wish that I had your business acumen,' Neil said, the sincerity evident in his voice.

'Ha ha! Don't flatter me, mister. Come on, you have a birthday party to DJ!' she said. 'Maybe you get to play some cool Punjabi tracks tonight.'

'God, have mercy on my soul,' said Neil with terror in his eyes.

The birthday party in question was that of Bunty Gulati, a man-child turning twenty-five years old on the premises of Kapital with an extravagant, daddy-sponsored birthday party. For Neil, Bunty seemed like a rich spoiled kid who wanted to burn unnecessary money. But for Sameera, Bunty was a living, breathing cash cow, and Kapital was in dire need of one.

'Just play whatever the crowd demands,' Sameera had instructed Neil along with the other members of the staff before the party had begun. 'We have only one agenda for the night. Keep the suckers happy and make sure they consume a lot of alcohol and generate a long bill.'

Everybody nodded their heads in agreement and got down to work.

Bunty arrived at The Grand Majestic Hotel in an olive-green Porsche 911 car, a colossal red ribbon flower donned over its bonnet. Bunty's friends, armed with their smartphone cameras flashing, waited for him at the entrance, making sure that every second of his entry was live streamed across all their social media. An additional drone camera had been deployed in the air to capture a bird's eye view of the ongoing birthday celebration.

'If birthdays are like this, I wonder what the scale of weddings in Delhi is,' Neil wondered out aloud. Both were watching Bunty's theatrics from the club's window.

'You have no idea. Delhi weddings are in another league altogether,' Sameera told him.

'I can imagine,' Neil said, his eyes transfixed on the birthday celebration that had begun on the ground floor.

'Looks like the birthday boy is going to enter the building. I think it's time for you to get on the stage and do your thing,' Sameera told Neil, nudging him by the arm.

'Wish me luck,' said Neil.

Neil estimated that about 150 people were a part of this party. When he himself was twenty-five he did not have more than fifteen friends by a far stretch. Come to think of it, as of today, at the age of twenty-nine, that number was in single digits. Phew!

The party had reached full swing in the span of an hour. The bartenders had been kept busy by the party-goers. Rivers of whiskey and vodka had flowed. A variety of shots, in different colours, and in different shapes of glasses were circulated around the party. Blue kamikaze shots in thin test-tube glasses seemed to be a hit and were the most in demand. To Neil's delight, the crowd was surprisingly receptive to his music. He was enjoying playing for them.

A group of four boys, all wearing blingy, colourful Gucci T-shirts followed Bunty around the club like his personal security detail. The Gucci Gang drank when Bunty drank, which was very often. They danced when he danced. They ate when he ate. At the stroke of midnight, the cake was brought in. It was shaped like a pair of bountiful breasts. All the birthday party attendees, girls and boys alike, gathered around to make sure that they were clicked with the cake. A sword (a real sword), akin to something that Neil had witnessed in *Game of Thrones*, was produced from somewhere. Bunty got himself photographed with the sword making silly poses. He then proceeded to cut the cake at the cleavage with the sword. The Gucci Gang fed him pieces of the cake before smashing his face into the breasts.

Neil found Sameera hanging by the bar area.

'So, your cash cow turned out to be a good bet,' he told her.

'It did!' she said.

'The club seems to have done an incredible amount of business tonight,' he said.

'It did!' said Sameera, her words slurred.

'Sam, are you drunk?' asked Neil.

'A little bit,' replied Sameera.

'Wow! What happened to your no-drinking-while-working policy?' asked Neil, as he sat down on the bar stool next to her.

'I make the rulessss. I break the rulessss!' she slurred.

'Fair enough,' said Neil. He asked the bartender for water, which he made her drink, holding the glass steady in his hands as she took small sips.

'Sam, you've done a great job organizing the party. But you should go back to your Suite now and have some rest. I'll ask Gyan Singh to escort you back,' said Neil and Sameera nodded at this suggestion. Neil dialled Gyan Singh and explained the situation to him.

'Gyan Singh is coming right up from the lobby. Also, I really need to take a leak. You stay here. Don't move. I am going to be back in two,' he told her and went towards the men's room which was located on the other side of the club.

Sameera laid her head down at the bar table. She felt somebody take the seat next to her.

'Hello, how are you doing there?' the person asked.

'Gyan Singh, that was quick,' said Sameera.

'It is me, Bunty!' said the person.

Sameera sat upright to find that it was indeed Bunty Gulati, the cash-cow-birthday-boy, sitting next to her.

'Hello, Buntyyy! How are you enjoying your birthdayyy partayyy?' she asked him, her words garbling and dragging.

'The party is awesome, Sameera,' said Bunty. "The other day when I had come with my dad to book the club, I knew that I had to celebrate my birthday here and nowhere else!'

'Thank youuuu! It honestly meaaans a lottt! Like a lottt!' said Sameera, holding her hands wide to emphasise on 'lot.'

'I have to confess that I have been a big fan of yours for many many years!' said Bunty.

Sameera was taken aback by his comment.

'My fan? Why? And how?'

'It started with a newspaper article five years ago in the *Business Tomorrow Times*. The article predicted that an inexperienced twenty-two-year-old Sameera Kapoor would not be able to control the hotel, and the nightclub business left behind by her deceased mother!'

Sameera burst out laughing. 'Trust me, that wasn't the only article that said that. I encounter such nasty articles even today. But you can't keep dogs from barking, can you?'

'And that's what I admire about you. Your ballsy attitude. Let's cheers to that, shall we?' said Bunty, giving her a shot glass filled with a transparent liquid, its rim lined with salt.

'I'm sorry,' said Sameera, gently pushing his hand away.

'But I shouldn't be drinking anymore.'

'Come on, I insist! It's my birthday. Just one shot,' Bunty was adamant. *'Ek se kuch nahi hoga* [One (shot) won't affect anything].'

'Okay fine, just one shot and one shot only!' said Sameera.

'Gentleman's promise!' said Bunty, bringing his pinky finger up, which Sameera reluctantly interlocked with her own.

Both of them clinked their glasses in cheers and gulped their respective drinks down their throats. Bunty seemed as normal as he was before drinking the shot, whereas there was a visible discomfort on Sameera's face.

'Time for a selfie with the birthday boy!' said Bunty, taking his phone out despite the evident distress shown by Sameera in her composure.

'No . . . I should leave!' she tried to tell him.

'Just after a few selfies!' he told her. 'See, I have some fun filters on my phone!'

Bunty's front camera had a Disney filter on. He made Sameera look into the camera and the filter made her eyes turn big and googly, and her skin soft and supple like a baby on the screen. Bunty got himself into the frame, joining his head with hers, and the filter did its magic on him too. Bunty clicked a few pictures.

'I should leave now, Bunty,' said Sameera trying to get up from the chair.

Bunty placed his hand firmly on her shoulders, pushing her down into the barstool and said, 'What's the hurry? Check out this next filter!'

The next was a dog filter. It gave both of them big dog ears, noses and tongues. Bunty clicked a few pictures.

'I am leaving, Bunty!' asserted Sameera in protest.

'Just one last photograph, I promise! We have to come closer for this one,' said Bunty, holding her by the arm.

The next was a heart filter. Both had to join their heads in a slant for the filter to make it look like they are the two halves of a heart. Bunty forced Sameera's face into the frame, and the filter made a heart as expected. And then, instead of clicking the picture, he kissed her.

13

Party Pooper

A flurry of different thoughts entered Sameera's mind. 'Where was Neil? Where was Gyan Singh? Where am I? What exactly is happening to me? And where is that foul stench coming from?'

She opened her eyes to realize that the foul stench was coming from Bunty, whose lips were locked in with hers ferociously. There was laughter, giggles and cheering in the background, but Sameera's mind couldn't place any of it properly.

'Focus Sameera, focus! Remember your taekwondo training.' A voice spoke in the quiet chambers of her mind. 'Bring complete attention to your body. Feel every bone and muscle within you. There is a deep power that is floating in your spirit. Summon that power and bring it to your knees. Now, at the count of three, kick the bastard with the energy of a stallion. One . . . two . . . and three!'

There was a shrieking cry of pain, and just like that, Sameera was free from her worst nightmare. Bunty was standing in front of her, his hands cupped at his groin and unmistakable agony on his face.

'The bitch kicked me in the balls!' Bunty cried to his minions from the Gucci Gang.

Neil and Gyan Singh arrived at the scene, their timing similar to the police of 80s and 90s Bollywood movies, arriving mere seconds later than their utility.

'Sam, what happened? Are you okay?' Neil asked a distraught Sameera whose spirit was almost at a breaking point.

'Boss Madam, tell me what happened!' Gyan Singh asked, uncharacteristically furious.

'That bastard kissed me forcefully!' she said pointing to Bunty.

'What the hell!' Neil exclaimed, his blood boiling with rage.

Neil went ahead, pulled Bunty by the collar and delivered a tight slap on the face. Neil's next attempt at the offensive was blocked by a member of the Gucci Gang. Bunty delivered a neat sucker punch on Neil's stomach.

At this point, Gyan Singh entered the brawl, pushing and shoving other members of the Gucci Gang around, like the Hulk squishing humans and aliens alike in *Avengers*. More people from the party, Gucci or not, joined in the action. Neil and Gyan Singh soon found themselves outnumbered as an assorted gang of Burberry, Armani, Hackett and Ralph Laurens surrounded them.

Seeing the situation, Sameera swiftly called for the club bouncers, who should have been there now on their own as reinforcements to Neil and Gyan Singh. Four jacked bouncers, wearing black crew neck tees, came on the scene. Eleven minutes and several broken glasses and bruised faces later, much of the situation was taken under control. The party was over, and everybody was asked to leave. Bunty, who was being escorted out of the premises by two bouncers, commented, loud enough for everybody to hear, 'This is not fair! She kissed me first!'

'Take him away! This lying piece of crap!' said Sameera, matching Bunty's decibel level.

The two bouncers, who were each holding Bunty by the arm, hardened their grip, much to his disapproval.

'*Behenchod*, let go of me!' he told them both. 'You domestic dogs, go wag your dirty tails in front of your mistress.'

One particular bouncer out of the two, who did not like being called a dog, pushed Bunty forward a little too hard, causing him to have a fall and tearing his shirt in the process. An enraged Bunty got up from the floor and removed the remainder of his torn shirt, revealing his chiselled torso for everybody to see. He stepped on the Babylon bar stool next to him, and further onto the bar table. Half-naked with a bloody face, he seemed to be possessed by a demon-like energy when he spoke next.

'Who the hell you bastards think you are?' He asked, looking Sameera in the eye. *'Tum jaante nahi ho mera baap kaun hai* [You don't know who my father is]! I can buy this entire place and 100 others with my pocket money. You fucking losers!' he continued.

'Get this monkey off my bar,' Sameera instructed her bouncers.

'Don't you dare touch me, you peasants!' Bunty told them before they could even make a move. He then did something that would go on to be the most defining moment of his life. He pulled out a wad of five hundred rupee notes and tossed them in Sameera's direction. 'Thank you for your time. If you want more, you know where to find me.'

'I'll murder you, you fucking bastard!' said Neil, as he charged towards Bunty to deliver the final punch of the night.

Bunty's eyes squinted, the sharp blur of overlapping disco lights distorting his vision. When he saw Neil coming for him from afar, the muscles in his shoulders tensed. His throat dried up and his body froze in anticipatory shock. He was a deer caught in the headlights.

But before Neil could reach him, the thick glass beneath Bunty's feet cracked into jagged lines, the tension from his weight and audacity being a little much to bear. Bunty came crashing down, his shenanigans for the night ending in an inglorious anti-climax.

14

Bling TV

The set buzzed with activity as a scatter of technicians and creatives hovered around. The showrunner wore a hat even though it was an indoor shoot. He saw the makeup artist do a light touch-up of the anchor and the two guests, who had paid good money to be on the show. When the make-up artist was done, he gave a thumbs up in the air, signaling it was time to go ahead.

'Shanaya, are you ready?' the showrunner asked on the handheld megaphone.

'Yes, sir,' said the anchor into the collar mic.

'Sameera and Neil, are you ready?'

'Yes.'

'Yes.'

'All right then. Lights! Camera! Rolling in 3 . . . 2 . . . 1 . . .! And action!'

'Hello! I am your host, Shanaya Malhotra, and I'd like to welcome you back to another episode of *Bling TV*, where we bring to you the latest offerings in your pursuit of fine living! I hope that you are having a bling week! Before we begin with today's episode, we would like to announce the winner from the previous episode's Bling Question. The question was:

'Which of the following is a luxury shoe brand? The options were:

A) Jamie Choo
B) Jimmy Choo
C) Jackie Choo
D) Johnny Choo

The correct answer obviously is "B) Jimmy Choo." And the winner of the Bling Question is Anita Gupta from Gwalior! Congratulations Anita! You have won an exclusive chocolate hamper from Chocotasy and vouchers worth Rs 50,000 from our associate brands.

'Now, moving on with today's episode, we have two very special guests with us in the studio, Ms Sameera Kapoor and Mr Neil Ramamurthy! For the uninitiated, Ms Kapoor is the owner of the famous Grand Majestic Hotel in Delhi, and she is also the brains behind the more famous, Kapital Club, which has taken Delhi's nightlife by storm. Mr Neil Ramamurthy is the resident DJ at Kapital. His music has been an instant hit with everybody who has been to the club recently. And he is a big reason why people want to keep coming back to Kapital! Welcome, Sameera and Neil to our show!'

'Thank you, Shanaya!' said Neil and Sameera in coordinated unison. The two of them were dressed up in business formals and seated on a couch, shooting for their first interview ever in the Film City in Noida. Pari Chadha, their marketing consultant, had arranged for this interview, and a bunch of others. 'Kapital needs to be heard and seen! It needs to cash in on its rising wave of popularity! Also, the few blips on its radar need to be undone!' Pari had told Sameera when the latter voiced her apprehensions about appearing for interviews.

'Okay, I'll do it, but I'll take Neil along with me to keep me company. I can't do this alone,' Sameera had told her.

'Sure! We can add an interesting narrative to his story. An American DJ, so fascinated with India that he drops everything to land a gig in Delhi. Watch how people will eat that up!' Pari had said excitedly.

And that was that. 'So, Sameera,' asked Shanaya, who occupied the single-seater sofa. 'How did you conceive the idea for Kapital?'

'Kapital was actually the brainchild of my parents, Harsh and Maya Kapoor. When they were young, wild and free, they got an idea to amp up the party scene in Delhi,' said Sameera, her eyes flitting back and forth, unsure of whether to focus on the host or the camera.

'So that's how Kapital started! I am just carrying the baton forward.'

'My next question is for you, Neil!' said Shanaya, naughty energy bubbling inside her as she made her switch from Sameera to Neil.

'Bring it on!' said Neil, a twinkle in his eye.

'So, Neil, you've lived in Boston and New York City all your life and have been in India for a few months now. Our viewers would like to know what is the one thing that you absolutely love about India?'

'You mean, apart from *Bling TV*?' said Neil and laughed at his own joke. Shanaya accompanied him with hearty laughter of her own. Sameera barely cracked a smile.

'Yes, what do you love about India apart from *Bling TV*, of course?' Shanaya asked him.

'India is beautiful! Everything about India is incredible—food, the culture, the vibe! BEAUU-TIFULLL!' remarked Neil, matching Shanaya's energy, oblivious to the tiny jealous frown from Sameera.

'So, Neil tell us about your experience DJing at Kapital?'

'Kapital is by far the best club I have ever played for in my life! The owner, Ms Kapoor,' Neil said pointing at Sameera, 'is amazing. She gives me the freedom to play my brand of music without trying to conform me to popular standards. So, yeah! I am enjoying my time playing music for Kapital.'

'Coming back to you, Sameera. Our viewers are excited about the upcoming events at Kapital. Could you shed some light on those?' asked Shanaya.

'With pleasure,' said Sameera. 'Kapital has a jam-packed calendar! We have the Spin Twins coming up to perform next Saturday! They are currently ranked as the fifty-fifth best DJs in the world, and it is their first gig in India. We are thrilled to host them! Apart from them, we have a mix of indie and international artists such as Be-Root, Triple Q, Panda Panda, Stayble and Punk-aj coming to perform later this year.'

'Wow! Now that is an enviable lineup of artists,' said Shanaya. 'I am sorry, but I have to ask you this. There are some rumours about Kapital floating on social media.'

Sameera felt her fists tighten and her heart beating faster as Shanaya elaborated on the rumours. But she was ready to address them. After all, it was a question planted on Pari's insistence to 'generate some positive PR for Kapital'. She had rehearsed the answer on her way to the studio.

'Some people claim that Kapital is jinxed. First, there was a fire on the opening night. Then, a boy was injured during a brawl not long after. Is there any merit to these claims?'

'I am glad you asked me this question. It gives me a chance to put all the rumours to rest, once and for all,' said Sameera confidently. 'Yes, there was a small fire on the opening night. But it was blown *way* out of proportion by the media. The fire was due to a technical glitch with the wires in the kitchen. Since then, everything has been upgraded. Trust me, Kapital is the safest place to party!'

'And what about that boy who was injured?'

'The only reason for his injury was he had partied a little too hard that night,' said Sameera, laughing in a bid to trivialize the issue. Neil tried to join in with the laughter but couldn't do it convincingly. Sameera continued, 'That boy slipped while dancing. That's very common if you ask me. In fact, I might have a dancing scar or two somewhere from a wild night out. Haha! The important thing is that he is doing fine now. In fact, he has come to Kapital quite a few times after the incident,' said Sameera, lying straight through her teeth on national television.

'That will be all from my side. Thank you, Sameera and Neil for a rocking interview! I am going to book my tickets for the Spin Twins playing next Saturday at Kapital,' said Shanaya.

'Thank you, Shanaya! It was great being on *Bling TV*. See you in Kapital next week!' said Sameera.

'Have a bling week!' said Neil, re-enacting *Bling TV*'s catchphrase, and causing Shanaya to look at him endearingly, while Sameera rolled her eyes.

Shanaya began with her closing act for the episode. 'Here is today's Bling Question for our viewers: What is the childhood nickname of this handsome Bollywood actor?'

A photograph of a bare-chested male actor coming out of the pool appeared on the screen behind Shanaya.

And your options are:

A) Bebo
B) Duggu
C) Lolo
D) Chi Chi

Fifteen minutes later, as Sameera descended the stairs of the studio, she received a text message on her phone.

(Pari) Seems like everything went according to plan.
(Sameera) Yes :) I have the best PR and Marketing manager in the world!

15

Brawl Veteran

'You sneaky bitch,' Emily's shrill voice echoed inside the Presidential Suite's living room. 'When were you going to tell me?'

'Soon-ish,' said Sameera to her best friend, who had a knack for knowing when she wasn't being 100 per cent honest with her.

'*Soonish*!' said Emily in a childish voice, making a mockery of Sameera's one-word answer.

'I am sorry, Em,' said Sameera. 'I should have told you as soon as Neil and I started dating again. You deserve to get a real-time update as you are my best friend in this whole universe!'

'Shut up with your fake flattery,' said Emily through iPad. 'And tell me, how often are you and Neil sleeping together? Spill the beans, girl!'

'We are taking it a little slow right now,' said Sameera.

The bedroom door opened behind Sameera and a sleepy Neil, donning a bedhead and clad only in a pair of boxers, came out rubbing his eyes.

'Babe, do you remember where I kept my toothbrush?' he asked her.

Sameera fully aware that Emily had caught her in a lie, turned red and only managed to say, 'I don't know, maybe check in the bathroom cabinet.'

Neil went back inside the room, while Emily had a wicked smile on her face. Before she could say anything, Sameera herself conceded.

'Okay, you've caught me. Neil has moved in with me in the Presidential Suite. Now you can wipe that smug smirk off from your face.'

'Well, well, well! Nothing can ever be hidden from the eyes of Detective Emily Johnson!' said Emily, grinning from ear to ear.

'Don't give yourself too much credit! You were just lucky that Neil came out at the exact time that I was talking to you,' said Sameera, her annoyance at her friend's gloating increasing with every passing second.

'Was it really luck?' Emily asked, raising a brow. 'Or was it the universe's carefully orchestrated plan to keep you from lying to me?'

'Very funny,' said Sameera, disclaiming her friend's outlandish theory.

'So, now that all your secrets are out in the open, tell me, when did the magic happen?' asked Emily.

'Do you remember I told you about the brawl in Kapital a couple of weeks ago?' asked Sameera, realizing that there was no point in keeping secrets from Emily.

'The one where that disgusting birthday boy forced himself on you? Yes, I remember!' said Emily, repulsion leaking into her voice.

'Yes, that's the one,' Sameera sighed. 'It was a mess after that. A grand mess.'

'I can imagine.'

'But thank god for Neil! I don't know what would have happened if he hadn't stepped up that night!'

'Stepped up how?' Emily was curious and made no attempts to hide it.

'He just took charge of the entire situation like a pro! From arranging for an ambulance to defusing the situation, he just did it so effortlessly,' said Sameera.

'An ambulance? For that disgusting birthday boy? He should have been left rotting by himself,' said Emily.

'That was my exact opinion as well. But Neil, a veteran of many club brawls, recommended that "we need to disqualify any future liabilities right now",' said Sameera, using finger quotes for emphasis.

'That seems the sensible thing to do, now that I think of it,' admitted Emily.

'I know, right?' Sameera continued. 'Anyway, the other people involved in the brawl were handed over to the police, who let them off the hook with a warning. Thanks to their well-connected families.'

'Oh my god! That is so bloody unfair,' said Emily.

'It is, but such is life. That night, during the chaos, I was still reeling from the shock, but Neil stood behind me, rock solid in his support.' Sameera's voice had gotten heavy from recounting the events from that night.

'Neil is perfect for you! Don't you dare break his heart this time,' said Emily, who was a tad emotional herself after listening to her friend's ordeal.

'Yes, ma'am,' said Sameera shifting to her happy voice. 'He is a keeper!'

'Sorry to bring that piece of human crap up again, but what happened to Bunty? Did he survive the fall?' asked Emily.

'Unfortunately, yes. The medics were prompt and resourceful. He spent a couple of days in the hospital for the concussion,' said Sameera with remorse.

'There is a cure for concussion, but none for being an asshole pervert,' exclaimed Emily, and the both of them sighed.

'True that,' said Sameera.

'How is the prep coming along for the Spin Twins?' asked Emily, moving on to the next topic for discussion.

'Oh my god, Em. It's insane! I have never seen a crazier response to anything ever in my life,' said Sameera, radiating euphoria and enthusiasm.

'Really? That sounds awesome!'

'It is! We are really excited about this. And you know what? All the passes sold out within four hours,' said Sameera animatedly.

'Four hours! That is bonkers, babe,' said Emily.

'Yes, indeed! Some of the other nightclubs tried to organize celebrity DJ nights of their own on the same dates, but I last heard that they are struggling to sell passes,' beamed a happy Sameera.

'This is insane. Everybody should watch out for Sameera Kapoor, the formidable boss of Delhi's discos,' said Emily.

The door opened behind Sameera again, and Neil walked out, this time clad in faded blue jeans and a tank top.

'Sam, have you seen my Apple Watch charger anywhere?' he asked as he scanned the living room.

'Okay, Emily! Seems like I gotta go now. My *boyfriend* needs my help in starting his day,' said Sameera, feeling weird and liberated at the same time at the use of the word 'boyfriend'.

'Not so easily. You have to introduce me to Neil,' said Emily, shrugging her shoulders.

'Next time. Not today. I really gotta go,' said Sameera, at the cusp of ending the FaceTime call, when Neil came into the frame from behind her.

'I heard that somebody wants to be introduced to me,' he said, looking into the screen at Emily before giving a small peck on Sameera's cheek.

'Hi, Neil! Finally, a formal introduction even though it is digital,' said Emily, grinning from ear to ear.

'Hi, Emily! Nice to finally meet you too. Sameera never stops talking about you,' said Neil, gently pushing Sameera's face aside so that he could look at Emily properly on the screen.

'And with me, it is all about you,' said Emily, as she looked at Sameera's passive-aggressive cue to cut the call. 'It is my bedtime here in Vancouver now! I will catch up with you two lovebirds really soon! Till then take good care of my girl!'

'Your wish is my command,' said Neil.

'Bye, good night! And good morning to your part of the world!' said Emily.

'Good night!'

'Good night!'

It was late at night. Sameera was curled up next to Neil, sleeping. Neil, who had had an Americano after dinner, a bad decision in hindsight, was wide awake. He wanted to go out for a walk in the lovely night weather outside but decided against it since it would involve moving Sameera from her current position of comfort. His phone dinged from the bedside table. It could only be one person. The other woman in his life. He took a deep breath before picking his phone up.

(Maa) I hope you are eating properly there in India
(Neil) Yes, Maa!!!
(Maa) Make sure that you eat your veggies too. Too much chicken will deplete your body of fibre

(Neil) Yes, Maa! I am eating all my veggies

(Maa) Also make sure that you are only drinking mineral water. Don't drink tap water. Your stomach is sensitive

(Neil) You've already mentioned this before! I am having ONLY mineral water

(Maa) Good! And don't even think of trying sea food. It doesn't suit you

(Neil) Yes, Maa

(Maa) Good!

(Neil) Maa, I miss you!

(Maa) I miss you too, my sweet child!

(Neil) Guess what, Maa?

(Maa) What dear?

(Neil) I didn't pop the question yet, but we are back together!

(Maa) That is the best news, my dear! When are you making me talk to my daughter-in-law?

(Neil) Calm down, Maa. She hasn't accepted my proposal yet

(Maa) But she will! You are such a sweet little boy

(Neil) Oof, Maa! I am sweet all right, but please don't call me little. I am 29 for god's sake

(Maa) You will always be my little boy!

He smiled.

(Neil) I'll make you talk to her soon. But I am taking it slow, right now.

(Maa) Good thinking.

(Neil) I am going off to sleep, Maa! Will talk to you soon

(Maa) Goodnight, my sweet little boy!

(Neil) Good night, Maa! Love you

(Maa) Love you too

16

Snooping

Dear Diary,

The past few days have been really busy at the hotel. Both Saba, my restaurant; and Kapital, Sameera's club, have been churning out incredible business. I see less and less of Sameera these days, and to my surprise, that doesn't bother me. Okay, that is only the half-truth. The reality is that the more I immerse myself in work, the saner I feel. I went on Google (again!) and dived into the rabbit hole of how to alleviate symptoms of a psychotic episode. I came across a video of a shrink in a suit and bowtie, whose YouTube page is literally called Bowtie Shrink. Among the many methods listed by him, I particularly found one interesting. Dive deep into the abyss of your mind and recall the most vivid memories from your past. These memories hold the key to unlocking the mystery behind your psychotic episodes.' This makes sense. I have so many of these vivid memories that keep replaying in my head every night in bed. I guess that if I wrote them down here, they would leave me alone and finally let me sleep in peace. So here goes nothing!

In my early days as a junior chef at The Grand Majestic Hotel, Harsh and Maya Kapoor would often come to dine at Saba late in the evenings. The corner window side table, with the silhouette of India Gate as the view, would be permanently reserved for them after 7 p.m. I would watch them from the sidelines, engaged in animated conversations and never getting enough of each other. It made me jealous. Two beautiful people in love and enjoying each other's company. Just like those Hollywood movies that create an unrealistic expectation of love. That was the life I wanted for myself. With Maya.

As the years passed by, I was promoted to the sous chef, the second-in-command in the kitchen. Things were going superbly for me. And as fate would have it, I began to see cracks in Harsh and Maya's marriage. Their late-evening dinner dates became less frequent. And on the off chance, if those did happen, they had completely lost their charm. It felt like I was looking at a pair of strangers quietly chewing the food kept in front of them. Had the honeymoon effect finally worn off? Harsh had gained a significant amount of weight and abandoned the rugged handsomeness of his youth. He was addicted to whiskey, cigars and women. There were whispers of his affairs in the bedrooms of The Grand Majestic Hotel. It became an open secret. I guess Sameera knew about them as well, but she chose to turn a blind eye.

Maya, on the other hand, had kept a tight grip on her youth and beauty. She spent hours and hours at the spa and the gym. She wore the most fashionable clothes and carried herself like nothing short of a film star! She kept herself busy with social events, both as an organizer and as an attendee. Exhibitions, fashion weeks, charity cocktails, sundowners and grand openings of luxury stores; her calendar was always full. I'm sure that the hyper-busy schedule was a way of avoiding her husband. The only time I ever saw the husband and wife together was when they were at Kapital, a club they had started with a lot of passion. It was the only glue holding their marriage together, apart from their daughter Sameera, who had been shipped off to a boarding school in Dehradun as soon as she was a preteen.

One awful day, Maya came to the restaurant in the afternoon, accompanied by a lady, probably a socialite friend of hers. She caught hold of a poor waiter right at the entrance and demanded,

'Is my regular table available right now?'

I watched the colour drain from his face as he stuttered to give an incoherent answer. 'The table is . . . there is somebody . . . the table . . .'

'What gibberish are you talking?' she remarked and walked straight into the restaurant.

It did not take her long to figure the reason out for the young server's scattered speech. Harsh was sitting at the bar stools across from their regular table, sipping red wine with a white girl who was wearing a dress with a deep plunging neckline. Harsh had cracked a joke that made the girl burst into laughter. Harsh's hand stroked her on the thighs, which she didn't seem to mind in the least.

Maya watched the spectacle from a distance, while her friend and the restaurant's staff waited for her reaction. A scene was to unfold in a bit. There would be yelling and crying. Accusations, ultimatums and finger-pointing. All this with maybe a dash of violence. But Maya managed to surprise every single one of the spectators, including myself. She turned to her friend and casually said, 'Babe, I am in the mood for sushi. Come I'll take you to this nice sushi place in Khan Market.'

The friend just nodded and followed Maya as she walked off from the restaurant. Needless to say, Harsh Kapoor and his paramour remained oblivious to the developments happening around them.

For the next few days, I didn't see Maya Kapoor at all. She and her husband lived in the Presidential Suite, and hence it was common to spot them at some or the other part of the hotel. But it seemed like Maya had disappeared from the hotel altogether. I tried to spot her in the Page 3 section of the local newspaper, but she was nowhere to be seen. Very odd. Maybe she had been taken sick and confined herself to her suite. But there was no way for me to verify that. I asked a waiter who often went to the Presidential Suite to deliver room service if he had seen Maya Kapoor. His (predictable) reply was that he never saw either Harsh or Maya Kapoor because Gyan Singh, Harsh's personal assistant, would collect the tray of food at the entrance.

So where was Maya Kapoor really? I had to find out. Her absence was killing me. I decided that it was time for me to give the Presidential Suite a little visit. The opportunity soon presented itself.

Upon the next room service order from Harsh Kapoor, I quickly assigned myself to the delivery. It raised an eyebrow or two in the kitchen, sure, but since it was Mr Kapoor's order, nobody thought a lot about it. I stepped out from the lift carrying a tray of the dinner order. As expected, I found Gyan Singh, Harsh Kapoor's loyal watchdog, wagging his tail by the entrance.

'Are all the servers on strike today?' he asked me, tongue-in-cheek.

'The owner of the hotel needs special service from a chef from time to time,' I said, tempted to stab him in the heart with the butter knife in the tray.

I expected a little bit more conversational to and fro between us, but Gyan Singh, never the talker, had a different plan altogether. He swooped on the tray from my hands like an eagle taking on prey in one swift move. And without uttering a single word, he turned around and marched towards the gigantic door of the Presidential Suite like the loyal dog he was. I had often wondered how and when Gyan Singh had come to be under the employment of the Kapoors. How much money did they pay at the pet store? An old bellboy told me that Gyan Singh's father began as a gardener for the Grand Majestic Hotel during Harsh Kapoor's father's time. Seeing his potential and commitment to work, he was quickly elevated to the post of PA. After his death, his son, Gyan Singh, took premature retirement from the army, and offered his services to the Kapoor family. As if they needed another servant to lick their boots.

Gyan Singh pressed the bell and a few seconds later the door opened. Harsh Kapoor stood there wearing a white bathrobe which carried his initials 'HK' monogrammed on the heart.

'Boss! Mr Kapoor!' I called out.

'Uh, Chef . . . Chef Alex!' he was startled to see me.

I told him I wanted to speak regarding an urgent matter about the restaurant before his loyal dog would shoo me away. Mr Kapoor, glancing at his Rolex, told me that he would swing by in an hour. I told him that it was urgent and that it must be addressed now and here. The desperation in my voice must have done the trick because he let me in with a sigh.

Gyan Singh grunted at his failure to keep me out while I let myself in.

'So, what is it that cannot wait?' Harsh Kapoor asked me once we were both seated opposite each other in the living room. Before I answered, I scanned the room briefly for any signs of Maya. There were none.

'The restaurant is in serious trouble,' I said. Now, I had a grand total of 1.5 seconds to think of a peculiar and exaggerated story to rationalize my presence on his expensive sofa. Else I was toast. I would be fired for being eccentric.

'And why is that?' he asked, his tone containing a tablespoon of irritation and a small teaspoon of curiosity.

I told him the head chef, Rajan, was stealing from the restaurant. I don't know why I said that. Was I finally giving voice to my deep-rooted envy towards Rajan?

'Stealing how?' asked Harsh, his interest in this conversation ignited.

'I am not sure, but I have a strong hunch that he is manipulating the register,' I said, thinking of the most obvious way somebody can steal from a restaurant. These were the days when fancy CRM software and CCTVs were yet to become the market norm.

Harsh Kapoor didn't say anything. He closed his eyes and thought for a while. It felt like an eternity.

He asked me if I had any proof when he finally opened his eyes.

'He is very careful when he is manipulating the cash and receipts. But I suspect that something is not right.

Even when we are overbooked by customers, it does not reflect in the sale register,' I said.

Harsh assured me that he would look into it, and that was my cue to leave. But how could I? I had not yet snooped around the suite to look for his wife, the love of my life.

'Can I please use your washroom? It is urgent,' I said, raising my pinkie finger. It was career suicide to use your employer's washroom in his private space.

But extreme times require extreme measures. Ain't it?

Harsh Kapoor pointed towards one door out of the four in the living room, before himself disappearing into one. I could see that he had been put on a serious trail of thought by my information. I opened the door to come across a carpeted bedroom. The room and washroom were both empty. I did a quick recce of the walk-in closet on an impulse, and boy! It was the biggest collection of clothes I had ever seen in my life. Suits, dresses, shoes, and whatnot! My entire family combined owned fewer clothes than this closet.

'Focus, Alex!' I told myself.

I came out into the living room. There was no sign of my employer.

I quickly went in through the second door which opened into the private home theatre. It boasted of a white screen almost as big as the wall, flanked by two mega speakers and a cinema hall-type seating. I was sure that this entire system cost more than my two-year salary. The home theatre was empty. Only one more room left to check.

The door was locked, but the key was still left in the lock outside. I turned the key gently and sneaked through. It seemed as if somebody had been living there. The bed was unmade. A woman's clothes lay strewn on the single-seater sofa chair. The bathroom was empty. So was the walk-in closet. No sign of Maya anywhere. What a waste of effort this was. I was almost on my out when I heard a distinct sound from the washroom. But how could it be? I tip-toed inside. The sound came from the shower enclosure, whose bottom half was shielded by a layer of frosted glass. I opened the enclosure and there she was. Sitting cross-legged on the floor, naked and crying; her body covered in black and blue bruises. Maya, my Maya!

17

Spin Twins

'Woohoo! This is a shoutout to all of you, PC fans! This is your favourite girl, Pari Chadha live on Instagram. I am at the capital of dance and music, Kapitaaaal!!!'

Pari's camera was in selfie mode, and she swirled a full 360° to give her audience a panoramic view of the club, packed right up to the hilt. Party-goers, with their drinks in one hand and the other hand up in the air, gyrated to the electronic music blasting from the speakers.

Pari's camera shifted its focus to the DJ stage where two ridiculously fit men sporting crew cuts and tight V-neck t-shirts operated the mixing console. They were almost identical; the only difference being how they preferred their facial hair. One had a goatee, a dark soul patch under his lips, and the other a neat French beard.

'Guess who is playing here tonight? Yes, you got that right! The Spin Twins are here all the way from

Hungarrrrrryy!' Pari announced to all her followers on Instagram Live, her voice soaring to a high, energetic pitch, tinged with excitement.

Gyan Singh sat at the corner of the Olympus Bar, sipping on his fourth single malt whiskey-on-the-rocks. He stared at an old black-and-white photograph of a tall turbaned teenage boy in loose capri shorts and sports t-shirt, and a short girl in salwar kameez standing in front of a large banyan tree, in his wallet. The boy held a basketball in his hands, a frown on his face and looked away from the camera. The girl seemed chirpy and gave a wide goofy smile. As the Spin Twins came on the stage, he folded the wallet and tucked it back into his pocket. Tonight, he had decided to cash in on the exclusive privilege that Sameera had given him since the resurgence of Kapital—food and alcohol on the house on his off days. Today was his day off and he felt like he needed a whiskey or four. Ahh! This was the good stuff. Unlike the cheap roadside sewage, he was otherwise accustomed to having. He couldn't even pronounce the name of this bottle, but he knew that he had found the elixir of life. He was certainly enjoying himself despite having to sit through the lyrics-less music the youngsters of today seemed to love so much.

'Kids in Africa would rather starve themselves to death than eat this crap that you call food!' barked Chef Alex, as a junior chef, with his head bowed down in shame, stood in front of him in the kitchen.

'Throw this garbage in the dustbin and cook it again. Every single dish that leaves through this kitchen has to be bloody fantastic. If any of you cannot meet those standards then take your sorry asses to a street dhaba. I don't want you here.'

Chef Alex made his usual rounds of the kitchen while everybody got down to doing their jobs. The crowd for the Spin Twins had ensured that this was the busiest night in the kitchen so far.

'To be really honest, I kind of underestimated the hype around the Spin Twins,' admitted Sameera.

'You did what?' Neil almost choked on his gin and tonic.

'I thought they were some regular DJs who randomly became famous on YouTube because you know how easy it is to get famous these days,' said Sameera with nonchalance.

'Sameera, babe,' said Neil as he took her arm and dragged her to a side. 'Please make sure that nobody has heard you making that comment. These people worship Viktor and Sergei aka The Spin Twins. They will wreak havoc in your club if they find out that you disrespected their gods like that.'

'Okay, fine! I won't disrespect your gods. But please, stop with the melodrama,' Sameera said as she sipped on her vodka and cranberry cocktail. I actually owe it to the Spin Twins for the most successful night of business ever for Kapital.'

'Ahem! Don't you think some credit should go to your boyfriend too?' Neil chaffed at her.

'Of course, my darling,' said Sameera planting a big wet kiss on his cheek

'It all seems worth it now,' said Neil, gleefully soaking in the kiss.

'Tell me seriously,' asked Sameera. 'How did you even manage to convince them to play at Kapital? I mean ours is not even the biggest or the most successful club in Delhi right now.'

'Where there is a will, there is a way,' said Neil, his voice proud and smug. Sameera punched him playfully on the stomach.

'Answer me now!' she instructed him.

'Okay! Okay! Okay! But please stop with your violence,' said Neil, folding his hands around the gin and tonic. 'It is simple. I have a friend who has a friend who knows the manager of the Spin Twins. I just leveraged my connections to get them here for you, my love.'

'I love you,' said Sameera, giving him a peck on the lips.

'Love you more,' exclaimed Neil.

She looked into his eyes and smiled. Despite the deafening noise around them, she felt at peace with him. Things had a way of working out, after all.

'Ma'am, but what about my remuneration?' asked Neil.

'What remuneration?' she snapped at him.

'You know, the one for getting the Spin Twins to Kapital,' said Neil, mischief in his voice. 'Club Paradiso was ready to give me a bucketful of cash, but I chose Kapital.'

'Oh, that remuneration! I thought I could pay you in kind tonight,' said Sameera, reciprocating the mischief.

'I might take you up on your offer,' he said, winking at her.

'You better do, mister,' she said.

The music being played by the Spin Twins grew more intense with their successive tracks. One of the Twins persuaded the crowd to 'put your hands up' and kept repeating the phrase till everybody on the dance floor had both their hands up in the air. Meanwhile, the other Twin kept jumping up and down like an excited chimpanzee to further amp the audience up. It worked. The crowd treated both the brothers with hypnotic loyalty.

'Come on, let's enjoy the music that we have worked so hard to arrange,' said Neil, as he held Sameera's hand and led her to the middle of the dance floor, making his way through a swarm of sweaty people.

Dancing with Neil, Sameera lost track of time. One moment they were both yelling the entire three-word lyrics of a track along with the Spin Twins. The next moment, they were banging their heads aggressively to the beat. Neil pulled her aside and whispered in her ear, 'Need to go to the loo. Coming back in two minutes.'

Sameera wanted to tell him not to go because of what had happened the last time he had left her behind to go to the loo. But she could not shed her strong-independent-woman-who-needs-no-man image. So, she simply nodded and continued to groove to the music. It felt oddly liberating and relaxing. She was all by herself in a sea of unknown people. She could dance silly like she loved to and nobody would even bother. She wasn't Sameera Kapoor, the owner of Kapital and The Grand Majestic Hotel. She wasn't someone who had to bear the entire responsibility of managing her parents' legacy. In that moment, she was just Sameera. She was a girl who loved to dance with abandon. She was a girl in love with the most amazing man in the whole wide world. She felt something that she hadn't felt in days, maybe months. Fulfilled.

And then something happened. The lights, every single one of them, went off. Followed by the music.

There was a brief silence before the crowd went wild. Screaming. Shouting. Yelling. Sameera panicked harder than at any other time in her life.

Oh my god, something bad is happening again! she thought to herself.

A bright blinding light switched on directly above her head. It was difficult to see anywhere else while standing beneath it. Was it a dream? Was she dead? And then she heard her name being called out from speakers.

'Sameera Kapoor! Sameera Kapoor!'

It was Neil's voice. But where was he? Sameera tried hard to see if she could locate him, but the spotlight shining directly in her eyes didn't make it any easier.

'Sameera Kapoor, please could you join me on the stage along with Viktor and Sergei?' said Neil's voice through the speakers.

The people in front of Sameera moved aside so that she could have a clear walkway. Not knowing exactly what was happening, she walked to the stage and climbed up the steep stairs. Her heart was racing. She didn't know what was happening. Neither did the crowd. But the anticipation of entertainment from the ongoing events had kept them pacified for the time-being.

Sameera found herself on the top of the stage along with Neil and the Spin Twins, whom she had met briefly in the afternoon when she had personally received them at the lobby of the hotel.

'Ladies and gentlemen, please give it up for Sameera Kapoor! She is the sole reason that the Spin Twins are here performing at Kapital tonight!' said Neil energetically into the mic.

The crowd roared and cheered. Sameera didn't know what to do in situations like these except for blushing.

'Sameera Kapoor, everybody!' said Viktor, while his brother Sergei raised his arms as a cue for the crowd to cheer louder for Sameera.

'I didn't do anything at all. It was Neil who organized the whole thing,' said Sameera, but without a mic she was barely audible to the crowd.

When the applause had settled down a notch, she realized that the Spin Twins were no longer on the stage. It was only her and Neil. And Neil was down on a single knee.

'Sameera Kapoor, you and I have known each other for some time now. But it seems to me like I have known you for many lifetimes. I promise that this was the only cheesy Bollywood dialogue in my script for today,' said Neil, pausing midway in his speech, giving time for the audience to laugh at his joke, while Sameera stood in front of them, a bag of nerves.

'Sameera, I know I have asked you to marry me before, and you weren't ready then. It was my fault for having put you in that position so soon in our relationship. But today, standing in front of you, or rather bending on one knee in front of you, I want to ask you this question one more time,' said Neil, as there were cheerful murmurs from the crowd.

Pari Chadha was filming the entire proposal and streaming it live on her social media. She had made her way to the absolute front of the crowd, right next to the stage. Gyan Singh had pressed pause on the single malts for the night and was observing the proceedings with keen interest. Chef Alex had come out of the kitchen immediately when one of the servers had excitedly declared, 'Sameera ma'am has been called to the stage by the American boyfriend!' to all the members of the cooking staff.

'Sameera Kapoor, make me the luckiest man on this planet. Marry me, please?' asked Neil, the most important sentence of his script having a magical effect on the entire club.

A girl in the crowd yelled, 'Say yes! He is so cute!'

Neil produced the ring that he had been safeguarding ever since he landed in India. It was the same ring that he had presented to Sameera a few months ago in New York City on New Year's Eve. That time her answer had been 'no'. This time it was different.

'Yes!' said Sameera, a mix of emotions—happiness, excitement and sentiment, all heavy in her voice.

Neil put the ring on her finger and kissed her as the crowd cheered on.

The Spin Twins dedicated their next track to Sameera and Neil, the couple of the moment. They danced and kissed and had their eyes only for each other.

'Your next drink is on the house!' Sameera announced to everybody from the stage, which was met with more cheering than the time she accepted Neil's proposal.

Amidst the music and the brouhaha, a creaking sound was heard from above. Before anybody could point a finger at it, a heavy spotlight loosened from the ceiling, falling on the girl standing right below.

18

Capital with a K

The decade-old air-conditioner made Antarctica out of the 120 square feet office situated on the third floor of the Central Delhi Police Headquarters. Inspector Kiran Kumar or KK, as he preferred to be addressed, liked to keep the air-con running at all times, even when he was not in the office. The cold breezy air helped him to cool off after he had had an exhausting encounter with a self-entitled moron, which in recent times was very often. If KK could get a rupee each for the number of times someone had told him, 'My taxes pay for your government servant salary,' he would have accumulated several lakhs of rupees, which, considering the exorbitant cost of living in Delhi, wasn't a lot. He felt uneasy as he scrolled down a list of 'the best hair transplant clinics in Delhi' on a twentieth-century computer that depended on a

BSNL dial-up modem for internet. KK had realized that being a non-crooked cop in Delhi was reason enough to lose hair in his mid-thirties and have little means of cash-inflow to fund a transplant. Trapped in a vicious circle.

The bulky landline phone rang angrily on the desk.

'Hello, Inspector KK speaking.'

'KK, come to my office immediately,' his boss, CP Jaiswal, roared from the other end.

KK had an intuition that a lot of new work was going to be dumped on his shiny balding head. And his intuitions were seldom wrong. He closed all the tabs on his browser and got up from his chair with a grunt. When he left the office, he didn't bother shutting the AC off, because the civilian taxes that paid for his salary were also paying for the electricity bill.

'May I come in, sir?' asked KK as he stood at the entrance of an office that was significantly bigger and more spacious than his own.

'Come! Take a seat, KK,' said CP Jaiswal, a tall heavily built man with deep, brooding eyes. 'What can you tell me about the death of the girl at that discotheque? I am forgetting its name.'

'Kapital, sir!' said KK.

'Ah, yes! Kapital. Capital with K. I don't understand this generation of today. Capital with a C would have been easy and simple. But no! They wanted to overcomplicate things just for the sake of it,' said CP Jaiswal, looking mildly frustrated.

'I agree hundred and one per cent with you, sir,' said KK, who had realized early on in his career that the best way to climb up the hierarchy of job was through good old-fashioned arse-licking.

'So, how familiar are you with the case?' Jaiswal asked.

'Not too familiar, sir. I mean I saw the video that is being circulated on WhatsApp, but I really don't know anything else,' admitted KK.

'I see,' said the boss. 'I am putting you in charge of this case. I want you to find out everything about the incident and report your findings in a file.'

'Yes, sir!' said KK.

'Visit the location and file an incident report.'

'Yes, sir!'

'And KK, try to wrap this up fast. I have another case waiting for you!' said the boss.

'Yes, sir,' said KK, as he dismissed himself from the boss's office.

Once back in his own office, KK summoned Badri Prasad, his subordinate in rank, but with twenty-five more years of experience in the police force.

'Badri Prasad, have you ever been to a nightclub? To party?' asked KK as his junior, a middle-aged man with thick dyed black hair, entered his office and saluted in front of him.

'Party?' exclaimed Badri in surprise. 'Is it somebody's birthday today? I promised my wife to lay off the samosas, but I guess that one piece wouldn't hurt.'

'Not that kind of party, Badri. I am talking of a real fancy club—where the rich people go to party!' said KK, amused at the mention of 'samosas.'

Badri's face dropped, and his shoulders drooped. 'You are talking about Kapital, aren't you?'

'I am.'

'Boss, that place is haunted. I have heard rumours of unpleasant things happening there. Plus, I saw the video of the poor girl getting crushed under the light. Please don't take me there,' said Badri with his palms folded.

'Come on, Badri. Don't talk nonsense,' said KK, his voice firm and not in a mood to take 'no' for an answer. 'You are a policeman. Why do you believe in this haunted mumbo-jumbo? We will go to Kapital and investigate the case. And that is final!'

'Fine,' said Badri, conceding easily to his boss. 'But sir, did I ever tell you that back in the day, I was known to set the dance floor on fire, and impress the ladies with my moves?'

'Really? What happened to you then?' jibed KK.

'Age and arthritis,' quipped Badri, weakly.

19

Katastrophic

The Flight of the Disco Light

Delhi Glitz Staff
27 July 2025

In the latest shocking turn of events, Kapital, Delhi's OG party capital, has managed to make it to the headlines once again. This time the reason is more sinister than a fire or a brawl.

Kapital hosted the world-famous dashing duo of the Spin Twins last Saturday. The club saw an unprecedented turnout in numbers to watch the Hungarian DJs perform, ushering Kapital into a new era of electronic music, especially after its disastrous opening

night party. It was a fairytale evening
for Sameera Kapoor, the proprietor, who
was proposed to onstage by her American
boyfriend, Neil Ramamurthy. But barely a
few minutes into their engagement, a disco
light disengaged (pun not intended) itself
from the ceiling and fell onto the head of
a girl in the crowd. Catastrophic or in the
language of Kapital, 'Katastrophic'.

A source close to Ms Kapoor, who wishes
to stay anonymous, has informed us that she
is unfazed by the incident, and is actually
focused on planning her wedding and honeymoon
with her American fiancé. Ms Kapoor has denied
making a comment on this despite the numerous
attempts our team made to reach out to her.
It would be interesting to see what her next
plan of action is as this saga unfolds.

Meanwhile, it seems like Kapital is not
destined for a smooth take-off anytime soon.
In the unlikely event it does take off, do
not forget to carry your party helmets!

(*Delhi Glitz* is organizing a candlelight
march for the Kapital victim at India Gate
today at 8 p.m. Subscribe to our Instagram
and X pages to stay updated.)

'It was just an accident, babe! Don't think too much
into it,' said Emily to an inconsolable Sameera.

'That is precisely what I am trying to tell her too,' said Neil to Emily.

Sameera and Neil were seated opposite each other in the former's office in the Presidential Suite, while a red-eyed Emily, who had been woken up at 4 a.m. (Vancouver time), joined them through the iPad. Behind Sameera, who sat on the boss' chair, was a life-size family portrait of herself as a toddler, missing two front teeth. She was accompanied by both her parents in their youth, all smiling passionately for the camera. Beneath the portrait, on the back table was a miniature and detailed model of The Grand Majestic Hotel, kept inside a glass enclosure.

'Did you know that she was an only child?' asked Sameera, choking on her sentence. 'She had no siblings.'

'I didn't know that before today,' admitted Neil. 'Our communication was strictly professional.'

'I cannot forget the look on her father's face when he lit the funeral pyre. It is all my fault. I shouldn't have restarted Kapital again!' said Sameera, wallowing in self-pity.

'No, Sameera! It was not your fault! It was an unfortunate accident!' said Neil, assertively. 'It is unfair for you to take the blame.'

'He is right. You need to get the guilt out of your system, babe. It wasn't your fault,' said Emily.

'She was so young . . . Only twenty-three, and already so successful! And managed a company of her own . . .' said Sameera, paying no heed to the words of her fiancé and best friend.

'Sam, you are in shock right now. Please don't do this to yourself,' said Neil, gently rubbing her back to console her.

'Neil, but Pari was my friend! Of course, I am in shock! She was the reason why Kapital was gaining so much popularity. I owe everything to her,' said Sameera.

'I am sure Pari was a wonderful person,' chipped in Emily, having little context about Pari before this ongoing FaceTime call.

'Sam, you have to understand that the spotlight falling on Pari was a freak accident. It had nothing to do with you,' said Neil.

'You do realize that Kapital is now done for, right? Nobody will ever step foot in it, ever!' said Sameera.

'Nonsense!' said Emily. 'Do you know how many people end up dead in Niagara Falls every year? About a hundred!'

Sameera stayed silent, soaking up the completely made-up information given by her friend.

'And do you know, despite the hundred deaths every year, how many people visit Niagara Falls every year? Millions!' said Emily, throwing in more fake numbers to make her point.

Neil's phone rang. He picked it up and had a very brief conversation before hanging up.

'The call was from your Frankenstein's monster, Gyan Singh,' said Neil, instantly regretting the unnecessary joke during this ultra-serious situation.

'What did he say?' said Sameera, ignoring Neil's comment.

'Two things,' said Neil. 'One—he's been trying to reach you for some time but your phone is switched off. Two—he caught a bellboy watching a video of the 'incident' on his phone. It's all over the internet.'

'On the internet?' said Emily, who was wide awake now and completely invested in the mindboggling event in her best friend's life. 'Let me try looking it up,' she opened her laptop and pressed some keys and literally in less than thirty seconds, she said, 'Found it.' She played the video and pointed at the FaceTime call at the laptop so that Neil and Sameera could also see the video. It was captioned #ProposalFail. 1,03,342 views and counting.

The video began with a view of the DJ stage. Neil had just put the ring on Sameera's finger. There was a loud cheer from the crowd. The Spin Twins came back on the DJ stage. The camera panned towards the crowd who all seemed to be elated. Then Pari came onscreen, excited and pumped, holding a cocktail glass and dancing. Then there was a fast and continuous change in the camera angles coinciding with a sharp shriek for two milliseconds, after which the video turned blurry and finally stopped.

'I think we missed something,' said Emily, as she rewound the video and pressed pause at a specific time.

It was exactly when the spotlight hit Pari on the head. It was as clear as day. The footage was from Pari's phone itself. She had managed to livestream her own death on social media. There was complete silence at either end of the FaceTime call.

Emily switched back to selfie mode. And then Sameera said what Neil had probably figured out on his own.

'Pari was standing in front to record the proposal! Our proposal'

'Oh my god!' said Emily.

'This is my fault,' said Neil, his voice, sombre and grim, as he took on the baton of guilt passed on by Sameera.

'I had asked Pari to record the proposal. She was standing below that awful light to get a better angle at the recording. Oh my god! What have I done?'

'It is not your fault!' said Emily, who had not imagined that her night would turn out the way it did.

'Babe it is okay, you couldn't have known this before!' said Sameera, patting Neil's back gently while he was on the brink of tears. The consolee had become the consoler.

'I had been planning it for days. It was Pari who gave me the idea to involve the Spin Twins,' said Neil, visibly shaken.

'It is okay to be sad for the loss of your friend, but putting yourself in a state of guilt is just not fair. And not to mention, it is really unhealthy,' said Emily.

Neil's phone rang a second time. Seeing Gyan Singh's name pop on the screen, Sameera grabbed it and spoke to her man Friday, while Neil and Emily intently waited in suspense.

Sameera hung up the call. 'There are police officers waiting for us at Kapital.'

20

Elephant in the Room

Alex Matthews's Diary Entry, 27 July 2025

Dear Diary,

I am completely hooked on Bowtie Shrink's YouTube channel. I have devoured hours' worth of content already and I am contemplating purchasing a course, which is at an 80 per cent discount for a limited time, off his website. It seems like he gets me. His words help me get through with my day. Business is annoyingly slow and isn't expected to pick up anytime soon because of an incident that happened at Kapital. It is a blessing in disguise as it gives me more time to listen to Bowtie Shrink and dive into the interiors of my mind. My mood and sleep are already much improved. There has been a psychotic episode here and there, but hey, I am only human! Today I want to recall a happy memory from my past. It was a time when everything fell into place. It was a few days after I discovered Maya in the bathroom.

After my fake snitching to Harsh Kapoor, Rajan, the incumbent Head Chef found himself suddenly fired from the job without an explanation. And I being the second in command was automatically promoted to his position. It was bloody fantastic! It meant less work and more money. My only job was to make sure that my team cooked well, or rather, really bloody well. And I always got to take credit in the end. Don't get me wrong, I did cook sometimes. Especially, when somebody from my team made an extreme mess of their assigned dish. I did step in every now and then and led the way.

About three weeks later, I was taking a round in the kitchen when a waiter came rushing inside and informed me that Mrs Maya Kapoor was here in the restaurant and was sitting at her usual table by the window. But we had reserved that table for the German ambassador and his wife. He would be here any minute now.

I opened the kitchen door just a little to steal a glance at Maya. She was indeed sitting by herself at her usual table by the window, although sans Mr Kapoor. She looked radiant in an evening gown just like those gorgeous Hollywood heroines from the magazines. I had made up my mind. The Germans be damned!

'Give the Germans some other seat. Don't you dare make Miss Kapoor move from that table,' I gave the waiter an ultimatum. Being the boss was fun.

I waited for a few minutes before she had placed her dinner order before showing my face.

'A glass of red wine for the lady?' I asked her, holding an unopened bottle of Casas del Bosque, our most premium Chilean red wine.

She turned gently towards me and smiled. Oh, that smile! Chasing that smile had made me come all the way to The Grand Majestic Hotel and become a chef. I looked at her face for the first time since that fateful day in the Presidential Suite. Most of her bruises had faded away. She looked healthier and happier.

'Chef Alex, how pleasant to see you!' she said.

'The pleasure is mine, ma'am!' I said, standing by her table.

'Why don't you join me for dinner and give me company?' she asked, still smiling and making me go weak in the knees.

I told her that I would have had joined her if it weren't for the peak hours at the restaurant right now. God what an idiot I was! But it was important that I did not come across as too eager.

But she insisted and made a cute little puppy face, which I had seen her only make for Harsh many years ago. Of course I couldn't resist. Life gives you only so many opportunities.

I rushed to my locker to get rid of the chef whites and quickly changed into grey trousers and a crisp blue shirt. A generous spray of cologne later, I was date ready!

Maya was swirling her glass with a subtle movement of the wrist like a pro when I arrived.

'Earthy with a touch of fruity. Right in my territory,' she said, when I asked her how she liked it.

'I knew you would like it, ma'am,' I told her, as a server poured some of the same wine into my glass.

'Call me Maya, please. No ma'am or Miss Kapoor,' she told me in all seriousness.

I had been waiting to call her Maya for ages.

The food arrived. We conversed on a variety of topics, but the events of our previous meeting remained unaddressed.

She asked me how I was settling into the role of the head chef.

I told her that it was less work but a significantly bigger responsibility. Every single dish that left my kitchen would carry my name irrespective of whether I cooked it or not. That carried a downside, sure, but the upside was better pay and many compliments to the chef from happy customers. I couldn't complain.

'Can I be honest with you?' she asked, turning solemn.

'Of course!' I said, and my heart jumped to my mouth in anticipation of the words that were going to come out of her mouth. Maybe this was the moment when she would talk about that day.

'This sorbet sucks!' she said, putting the spoon down in the bowl and pushing it away. 'This is by far the worst sorbet I have ever had in my entire life, and I have had quite a few of them, mind you!'

'Shall I call for another dessert?' I asked, breathing a huge sigh of relief.

She asked me not to bother and that she would take me somewhere for much better dessert. Something 'truly mindblowing'. When I asked her where, she just told me to relax and trust her.

Half an hour later, we were parked in a night food street in Maya's Land Cruiser. Hawkers lined their makeshift stalls along the footpath and served their fares to people from every economic class of the city. It was around 11 p.m but the footfall in the area was completely maxed out. I had crossed this busy market area several times but had never actually stopped to eat.

'Isn't this the best dessert ever?' Maya asked from the driver's seat, as she dipped a white plastic spoon in a flimsy plastic glass and dug into the said dessert.

'Sure!' I said, looking at my own plastic glass and spoon, which had practically remained untouched.

'You have not even tasted yours!' she said, looking at my glass.

'Is it safe to eat?' I asked, looking at the sweating street hawkers from her window serving all kinds of foods without gloves and a complete disregard for any sanitary standards.

Maya looked at me as if I had asked her something really offensive. And then she burst out into a fit of hysterical laughter. She agreed that the *kulfi-falooda* was not made in a five-star kitchen such as mine, but she would take full responsibility for the fact that I won't die after eating it.

I took a leap of faith and dunked the spoon into the flesh of the frozen milk and vermicelli noodles, and carefully brought it into my mouth. Maya waited to see my reaction.

'It is delicious!' I finally said after the *kulfi* had completely melted into my mouth.

'You can tell me the truth.' She wasn't convinced.

I took a bigger bite and smiled my most authentic smile while the dessert wreaked havoc on my sensitive teeth inside. Only then did she let it go.

I told her that I had not taken her for somebody who enjoyed street food. She was taken aback by my comment and asked me to elaborate. I told her that because she was so high-society and sophisticated, it was hard to believe that she would be into a regular middle-class kind of a thing. She asked me if I was trying to call her snooty and was visibly offended. There was an awkward silence in which I tried to do a mental screening of my next words to her so as not to come across as a fool. I was livid with myself for ruining the night. What was I even thinking? Calling the woman that I have yearned and pined over for years, snooty! What was the best way to come across as genuinely apologetic and embarrassed?

Then, for the second time in five minutes, she burst out laughing and told me that she was just taking my case.

'You are wicked, Maya Kapoor!' I said.

'Thank you! I wear that title with pride,' she said, a smug smile on her face.

'Does Harsh also like street food?' I asked, and almost instantly regretted it. Her face lost its cheerfulness. The mood inside the Land Cruiser switched from romcom to tragic drama. If I had a gun, I would have simply shot myself in the brain and relieved myself of this situation. No kidding.

I apologized and told her that it wasn't any of my concern. She said that no it was okay, and it was anyway time to address the elephant in the room. I couldn't guage her voice though. Was it sombre? Angry? Not cheery, definitely.

I sat up straight and stiff, abandoning the glass of half-remaining kulfi in the cup holder, and geared myself for a difficult conversation.

She told me that it was an open secret that her marriage with Harsh was on the rocks. It had been for quite a while now. I told her that every marriage has its ups and downs, even though I had never been married myself. She told me that hers had turned really ugly. They had begun to resent each other. She knew all about the affairs, and how he was trying to mock her. She had pushed it all under the carpet, hoping it was all a phase. She didn't want her daughter, Sameera, to grow up in a broken home. But one day, Harsh crossed all limits.

The way Maya's eyes had swelled up, I braced myself to hear something disturbing.

One day she caught Harsh with a woman on their bed in the Presidential Suite. That was the end of her patience. She couldn't be insulted like that. Maya hit the woman and chased her out of her home. But she had never seen Harsh so angry. He called her all sorts of names and asked her to fuck off from The Grand Majestic Hotel—his property. The argument escalated and before she knew it, Harsh had slapped her on the face.

I could figure that this was becoming increasingly difficult for her to narrate. But she went on.

Harsh lost track of reality and hit her again and again, till she couldn't stand properly. After he recovered some sense of what he had done, she saw the look of fear in his eyes. He knew that he was in trouble. He pleaded for forgiveness. But she did not concede to his crocodile tears. Maya told him straight up that she would expose him for the monster that he was. The word 'monster' triggered him, and he hit her again. He dragged her and locked her inside the bedroom. He took her phone and even cut the landline.

Tears owed freely from her eyes and onto her cheeks. I wiped them with the paper napkins that came with the kulfi-falooda. I told her that it was okay, she didn't have to recount those terrifying details for me.

But she said that she wanted to. It was the only way to get it out of her mind, body and spirit. I asked her to go on then.

She was locked inside the bedroom for two days with no food, water or any contact from the outside world. She literally thought that she was going to die. On the third day, Harsh opened the door and brought her outside to the living room. He asked her to clean up and get ready because they had to attend his best friend's forty-eighth birthday party, which was being hosted at Kapital that day. But she had no energy to move, let alone get ready for the party. He dragged her inside the bathroom, stripped her naked and pushed her into the shower. She laid over there for hours and hours. She didn't have enough power inside her to get up and turn the shower on. Lying naked on the floor like that, she went into a dark place in her mind. She contemplated suicide. And she would have gone ahead with it too, if it weren't for me, who had come out of nowhere and helped her to her feet. She owed me her life, she told me.

She finished her monologue with a fresh stream of tears from her eyes. I brought a fresh napkin to her cheeks, but instead of letting me wipe her face, Maya pulled me closer. And kissed me.

21

Living Corpse

'Good afternoon, officers! How can we help you?' Neil asked, addressing the tall balding police officer and his sidekick.

'Hello! I am Inspector KK from the Delhi Police, and this is Constable Badri Prasad,' said KK, pointing towards his junior, whose amazement at being in a sophisticated night club with shiny disco lights and futuristic interior design had rendered him speechless.

'How can we help you?' Neil asked again, wanting to move beyond the pleasantries and get done with this while a distraught Sameera stood by his side.

'We want to speak to Miss Kapoor, the owner of this club,' said KK.

'I am Sameera Kapoor. What is this regarding?' asked Sameera, even though it was obvious that it had to be regarding Pari's death.

'We are here on a friendly visit, ma'am. We understand that there was an incident here last night,' said KK.

'Yes, there was an *accident* here last night,' said Sameera, placing a lot of emphasis on the word 'accident'. 'But the police were here immediately after it happened. And as far as I know, they are done with all their paperwork.'

'Yes ma'am, all the paperwork for the accident is indeed complete,' KK agreed with her.

'Then what are you here for?' Sameera snapped at the officer in a tone that would be interpreted as rude by most people.

Before KK had the chance to respond, Neil stepped in to defuse the situation.

'Listen officer, we appreciate that you have come to give us a visit. But please understand that we haven't been able to sleep all night because of the accident,' Neil said. 'And Sameera gets really disturbed after such events. So, please excuse us.'

'You said "such events" as in plural. Have there been any other disturbing events at this club? It seems like one coincidence too many,' said KK, trying to throw Neil off his feet.

'Absolutely not. It was a slip of the tongue,' said Neil, while Sameera took a step back and let him handle the situation. 'But what I am trying to say is that Sameera is really disturbed right now. It would be great if we could go and have some much-needed rest.'

'By all means, please go and take rest. The last thing I want to do is bother you,' said KK, not breaking eye contact with Neil.

'Thank you so much, officer,' said Neil, surprised at how easy it was.

'But I was hoping to work around and just absorb the beauty of this place if that is okay for you,' said KK, still making perfect eye contact and making Neil a tad uncomfortable.

Neil looked at Sameera to give the authorization.

'Of course, you are most welcome to look around,' said Sameera without meaning a single word of it.

'Thank you, I promise to be out of your hair in no time,' said KK.

'My personal assistant, Gyan Singh, will be here to accompany you in case you need anything,' she said, looking at her right-hand man.

'That is kind of you,' said KK.

Sameera and Neil walked towards the exit, leaving Gyan Singh to babysit the two policemen. Sameera muttered the words, 'Friendly visit, my foot,' when she was almost out of KK's earshot, half expecting KK to hear her.

KK heard the words loud and clear and smiled looking at Gyan Singh.

'Your boss is a very strong character, isn't she?' asked KK.

Gyan Singh did not reply.

'How long have you worked for Miss Kapoor, big fellow?' KK asked his second question, unbothered by the unanswered first.

There was no reply again.

'You aren't much of a talker. Now I see your value as a great employee,' said KK, walking up to Gyan Singh to maybe extract a reaction out of the man who was giving the guards outside Buckingham Palace a run for their money.

'Thirty years,' said Gyan Singh, suddenly and flatly.

'Ahh! So, you do speak!' said KK, bending his face upward to match Gyan Singh's gaze.

'Thirty years is a long time! But Miss Kapoor herself strikes me as a woman in her mid-twenties,' said KK.

'I worked for her parents,' said Gyan Singh, without any further elaboration.

'Aah! A loyal family servant,' said KK. 'You know, back in my ancestral village, we had several workers on the farm who had spent forty-plus years working for us. But alas! It is a different situation now.'

If that piece of information shared by KK seemed interesting to Gyan Singh, he did a brilliant job of not showing it. Or maybe he did not find it interesting at all. There was no telling with Gyan Singh.

'You like working for Miss Kapoor?' asked KK relentlessly, like a punching toy that always stood straight up, no matter how many times you hit it.

'She is a good boss. I like it here,' said Gyan Singh. Brief and to the point.

'And how is it working for that boyfriend of hers?'

'He is her fiancé now,' said Gyan Singh matter-of-factly.

'Ahh! Yes! Sorry, my bad. I was just looking at the proposal video on my way here. Let me rephrase this. How is it working for Miss Kapoor's fiancé?' asked KK.

'Mr Ramamurthy is not my boss. Miss Kapoor is,' said Gyan Singh.

'Okay, fair enough. How long have your boss and her fiancé been together for?' asked KK.

'Boss! Boss! Boss!' KK's assistant Badri, who had wandered off in the club on his own, shouted as he came running towards KK and Gyan Singh.

'What is it, Badri?' asked KK, irked that his subordinate had put a speed breaker in their less-than-free-flowing conversation.

'I found it! I found it!' Badri said, excited like a little kid at the candy shop.

'Found what, Badri?'

'I found the spot! The spot of the incident,' said Badri.

'That's great, but we were eventually going to find it anyway. It is not exactly a mystery. Remember, the police were here already last night,' said KK, to which Badri Prasad's face dimmed down as if he had just been refused candy by his father.

'Anyway, so where were we, Gyan Singh?' KK turned towards his interviewee only to discover that Gyan Singh had stealthily moved a few steps towards the exit and was talking discreetly on his mobile phone.

'There goes that conversation. I guess that we should look at the incident spot that you have discovered,' said KK turning to Badri, whose face lit up again. There was candy after all.

KK followed Badri as the latter led the way through the long corridor, which led to a big empty hall. KK was stunned looking at the club. It was magnificent. There was a stage in the centre with a dance floor all around it. The bar counter was longer and better stacked than the ones he was used to seeing. The whole set-up reminded him of a Bollywood song sequence where the hero danced with a bunch of scantily clad white girls. It was a club exactly like this. Maybe it was the same one. He would have to verify it on YouTube after this.

They walked around the main stage until they came across what Badri was too eager to show. A chalked human outline was drawn on the floor. Exactly above the outline, KK noticed that there was an unusually large empty space on the ceiling as compared to the rest of the area.

'This must be where the spotlight originally hung!' KK remarked standing directly beneath the spot.

'Ouch! It hurts to even think about dying like this!' said Badri, looking up at the empty ceiling spot and then down at the chalked outline.

'Badri! I have an idea! I want you to do something for me!' said KK, having a sudden brain wave.

'Yes sir, tell me!' said an excited Badri.

'Stand right underneath here,' said KK, nudging his junior beneath the exact spot of the missing disco light. 'Now I want you to imagine a big heavy weight falling on your head.'

'Okay, I am imagining that, sir!' said Badri channelling the energy of a kid at the candy store once again.

'Don't just imagine, give me a reaction as well. Show me where and how you will fall,' instructed KK.

'Aaah!' squealed Badri as he pretended that something very heavy hit his head and fell into the chalked silhouette of Pari Chadha.

KK walked around Badri's alive corpse and said, 'You are a very bad actor, but I want you to keep lying down and be still until I tell you otherwise.'

'Yes, sir!' said Badri, his face on the floor.

KK stopped walking and muttered to himself: *The floor-to-ceiling height must be at least 20 feet, and judging by these other lights, the piece that fell on the victim must be at least 15 kgs.*

KK stopped his analysis. Footsteps were approaching them. He could hear them becoming more audible as they came nearer. Finally, KK saw Gyan Singh emerge from the long corridor. Gyan Singh was flanked by two bulky men in black trousers and tight V-neck t-shirts of navy blue colour.

'I thought you didn't enjoy my company, Mr Gyan Singh,' remarked KK. 'But now you are back, and you have brought guests with you.'

'Miss Kapoor would like you to leave the premises,' said Gyan Singh, making it clear that he was the in-charge between him and KK.

'Can't we stay for a little while?' said KK in a childish voice.

'Your department has already conducted an initial investigation. Do you have a warrant for a further inspection?' Gyan Singh asked.

'No, but I . . .'

'Then leave!' said Gyan Singh, loud and clear and the bouncers flexed their muscles in a show of physical power.

'Get up, Badri. Time to go home,' said KK to his junior. 'Home, already?' exclaimed Badri, who was enjoying playing a corpse.

'Yes, get up. They won't let us stay without a warrant,' said KK.

'That sucks,' said Badri, as if the candy was snatched right from his mouth.

22

Brownie Points

'KK!' bellowed Jaiswal, as he entered his subordinate's office, bringing with him the smell of pan masala and talcum powder.

KK, who was browsing through the internet on his computer, was caught off guard. He jumped out of his chair.

'Jai Hind, sir!' said KK, bringing his right hand quickly to the forehead.

'Jai Hind,' reciprocated his boss. 'Did you finish working on the report?'

'The Kapital case?' asked KK.

'Which else?' the boss asked. He seemed to be in a mood. Probably argued with the Mrs in the morning, KK guessed.

'Sir, I am still working on it. I went for a visit seven days ago. But I need to conduct a thorough investigation,' said KK.

'KK, you are a good cop,' said Jaiswal, taking the chair opposite KK.

'Thank you, Sir,' said KK with a toothy smile, and easing into his own chair.

'But please do not make this case more complicated than it is,' said Jaiswal.

'I am due to retire within a few months. You already know that, don't you?'

KK nodded his head in affirmation. It was a rhetorical question. Of course, he knew about his boss's upcoming retirement. Jaiswal never missed an opportunity to talk about it, and his plan to finally meet his newborn grandson for the first time in London after leaving the police force. At this point, the whole Central Delhi Police Department knew about it.

'Don't make this any harder than it already is,' said Jaiswal. 'Just file your report and submit it. I want you to spend more time on important cases. There is an FIR against an online troll who sent death threats to an Indian bowler's two-year-old daughter because he conceded too many runs in the last over.'

'Yes, I know sir. I saw the match myself. What a shame! It seemed like the bowler had fixed the match. All he had to do was defend 22 runs in the last over of the semi-finals,' said KK, shaking his head as if this were a great personal tragedy for him.

'I see that you are already acquainted with the basic facts. I want you to lead the investigation into this. It is basically a slam-dunk case. The cyber-crimes unit will fish out the person for you. All you have to do is to nab him by the collar and take the credit. I want my department to solve all these high-profile cases before I leave. I want to retire on a high,' said the boss dreamily.

'Understood, sir! I will make sure that you retire on a high,' said KK pumping his boss up. Ass-licking 101.

'Good!' said the boss standing up. 'Wrap the Kapital report up and jump onto the next case before somebody else swoops it from your hands.'

'Yes, sir,' said KK, standing up as his boss walked out of his office.

KK sank back into his seat and opened an unfinished MS Word file titled 'The Kapital Death'. He gave the document a brief look and proceeded to write the following line in the end: "No foul play suspected in the accident."

The door of his office cabin opened and this time, Badri Prasad, his loyal sidekick, walked in holding a paper plate that contained two crisp samosas and a side of reddish-orange chutney.

'What's the occasion?' asked KK, looking at his favourite snack.

'It's from the man who had filed a missing person's report for his dementia-ridden father last week. Our department was able to locate the father wandering in a public park within four hours of the report. The man has sent samosas for the entire department in gratitude,' said Badri, as he handed the plate to his boss.

'On that note, let us hope his father gets lost a few more times,' said KK, as he took a bite of the piping hot samosa.

'Boss, when are we going to the disco next?' asked Badri when KK had completely devoured the first samosa.

'Maybe never,' came out the reply as KK dabbed the second samosa in the chutney.

'Why sir? Why not?' asked Badri.

'Because Jaiswal wants us to work on another case. Something to do with an online troll and a cricketer,' said KK as he chewed the food.

'Does that mean that we will get to go to a cricket stadium?' gleamed Badri.

'Forget about the stadium. I doubt that we will even get to meet the cricketer,' said KK.

'But why sir?' Badri's excitement level was taking a nosedive.

'Didn't you hear me? We need to find an online troll. All the work will be done on computers except for the final part where you will go and nab the culprit from his house!'

'What's the fun in that, sir? Besides, this operation seems more suited for the Cyber Cell. It seems like the big boss is trying to accumulate as many brownie points as he can before his retirement. I hate these open and shut cases,' said Badri.

KK smiled. 'Well, what can I do about this situation? I don't make the rules.'

There was a knock at the door before it opened a few inches and a peon, clad in loose khaki trousers and shirt, peeped in.

'What do you want?' asked Badri.

'This came for KK sir,' said the peon meekly, holding a sealed yellow A4 envelope in his hand.

'What is this? Who gave it to you?' enquired Badri.

'I don't know. The constable watchman handed it over to me,' said the peon.

'Wow! What better place than a police station to receive mysterious packages!' said Badri as he collected the package and handed it over to KK. The peon made himself scarce after making the delivery. KK ripped open the packet and withdrew a bunch of papers from inside it. Scrutinizing the pages properly, KK pushed back his chair and squared his shoulders.

'Badri, it's the time to disco! We are going to give Kapital a visit again!'

23

Relaxation 101

Alex Matthews's Dairy Entry, 4 August 2025

Dear Diary,

Sameera is gearing up to get things back to normal after the *incident*. I am pleasantly surprised by her leading-from-the-front attitude. After all the hiccups that she has seen at Kapital, it would be understandable if she took a step back and relaxed. But no! She wants to conquer all her ambitions, and that's what I love about her. The resilience in this girl reminds me of her mother. Same beauty, same brains No wonder I am enchanted, the second time over. Maybe I should recommend her Bowtie Shrink's breathing technique. The 4-7-8 technique to calm one's nerves down. Inhale for four seconds, hold for seven seconds and exhale for eight seconds. Repeat the entire system for a few minutes and you feel your nerves calmed down. You need to visualise something soothing to make this more effective. Like the waves smoothly washing up on the shore over and again. Or the sound of raindrops hitting the parapet while you are warmly tucked in bed with your partner. I always imagine Sameera as my partner for this exercise. I wonder, if I teach her this technique, will she imagine me too?

Before I continue my flashback story after Maya and I shared a kiss in her car, I would like to verify something for the benefit of the whole wide world. Yes, the stereotype is true. The stereotype of what you may ask? Well, the one of falling in love. Whenever I was with Maya, I felt like I was on top of the world. I imagined an orchestra of violinists serenading us at every given moment. Our affair was passionate, hormonal, and not to mention, super-duper secretive. Life was poetic. Life was beautiful. Life was Maya . . .

It was around 4 a.m. in the morning when Maya tried to wake me up. And quite vigorously at that.

'What is it, sweetheart?' I asked, still half-asleep.

'Wake up! Hurry!' she said.

I opened my eyes. The bedside lamp was on. Her hair was a mess. A sense of urgency radiated from her beautiful face.

She asked me to get dressed and leave, quick! But I was in a mood for a little romance. I asked her if anybody had ever told her that she looked even prettier when distressed as I took a lock of her hair and rolled it around my finger.

She nudged me in controlled aggression and told me that it was no time for my corny dialogues. I had to leave immediately because Harsh was on his way back.

I was properly awake now. My girlfriend's husband's name was enough to pump adrenaline into my system and propel me into a state of complete alertness. But how was this even possible? Wasn't Harsh supposed to be away on a business trip?

Maya told me that there was no time to explain. Harsh had apparently preponed his flight and was on his way to the Presidential Suite. She was terrified and shaking, but still looked like the prettiest woman in the world.

I sprang out of bed and got dressed in supersonic speed into my chef clothes, and probably broke a world record if such a category existed in the Guinness Book that I loved reading as a kid. Anyway, Maya threw me out of the Presidential Suite as soon as my naked body was clothed. I dashed barefoot through the empty corridor, my shoes dangling in my hands. Finally breathed a sigh of relief when I was in the elevator, and it began its voyage to the ground floor. But, as soon as the elevator doors opened to the hotel lobby, I stepped out only to collide with my employer and rival in love, Harsh Kapoor, who was stepping in.

'Alex Matthews, my star chef! So good to bump into you like this,' he said as he tried to wrap me in a bear hug. He reeked of whiskey and cigars.

'So good to see you too, sir!' I said, becoming self-conscious of any giveaways that indicated that I was just in bed with his wife a few minutes ago.

He asked me what was I doing at this hour? Taking my role as the Head Chef too seriously he assumed and poked my belly with his sausage-like thick fingers. The audacity. I should have had poisoned his black coffee the first day we met at Uncle Martin's restaurant.

I cooked up a story about a group of diplomats scheduled for breakfast at the restaurant in a few hours. It was plausible given how close Chanakyapuri was to the hotel. We always had diplomats, ambassadors and expats shuffling in and out.

Harsh's face turned from a jolly good fellow to that of an army general. He came ridiculously close to my face, nauseating me with his ridiculous stench.

He advised me to relax a little in life while I struggled to pause my inhaling mechanism. He questioned the point of my being in the restaurant at 4 a.m. when I was the boss of this place? I should have sent in a junior.

I thanked him for his (unsolicited) advice, but he was not done yet. He told me that since I was still a young man, I should be having more fun in life. Maybe, get a woman or two to keep me company at night.

The joke was on him because off late the only woman keeping me company at night was his wife.

After his free advice, I excused myself and let the moron stumble into the elevator. I came outside to the porch and inhaled a deep dose of oxygen-rich air. Oh dear! What a narrow escape!

A few hours later, I found myself standing amidst the bustle of the breakfast rush at the restaurant. It was only 6 a.m., but this place was high on energy. A pair of young Caucasian parents helplessly tried to feed fruit loops and milk to their twin toddlers who, sitting high on their baby chair thrones, made a grand mess of the food. A group of four Japanese sexagenarian men in lawn tennis gear engaged in a passionate discussion about something that was far beyond my comprehension. A suited gentleman, probably an expat, sat quietly by himself, reading a business newspaper and eating toast. I felt a pat on my back. I turned around to see Maya standing there like a breath of fresh air that she was.

'We need to talk,' she told me.

'Yes, of course, ma'am. Is the food satisfactory?' I asked, keeping up with my role as her employee in the public setting.

She did not play along and repeated that we needed to talk. Soon and in private. I took her aside near the cold storage room and asked her what was up.

'I think he knows,' she said.

'Knows what?' I asked, fully aware of where this was going

'Knows about us, the affair,' she said.

'He knows about me?' I asked in disbelief.

'Not you, per se, but he has a hunch that I am being unfaithful to him,' Maya said.

'But how is that possible?'

She told me that after I left, Harsh came to the Presidential Suite completely sloshed. I interrupted her to inform her that I had the privilege of bumping into him by the elevator just before that, giving a half-laugh. She ignored me and continued.

Upon seeing both sides of the bed were unmade, he became enraged. He called her a 'whore' and demanded to know where she had hidden her secret lover, as he rummaged through the entire suite in a fit of jealousy. The couch was turned upside down. Every room, bathroom and closet was frantically searched And when he found nobody anywhere, he held her arm so tight that she thought that he was going to murder her. She felt even more scared than the time he beat her black and blue and locked her inside the room.

Tears rolled down her cheeks as she stood in front of me. I pulled out my handkerchief and wiped them. I asked her not to cry and promised that we will find a way to be together.

She told me that she was scared. Scared for her life. What if Harsh lost all self-restraint while beating her one day? She didn't want to die, and she was tired living like this. More tears streamed down from her eyes.

I promised that I wasn't going to let anything happen to her, and that, I was going to march up to Harsh and tell him all about us. I would demand that he divorce her, and we could sail into the sunset like we always wanted to.

She told me that it was the worst idea ever. Harsh wasn't a rational man. He was a sadist who would do anything to see her suffer.

Maya rolled up her top's right sleeve. My blood boiled at the spectacle in front of me. The otherwise smooth and milky skin of her arm was now black, blue and swollen. I tried to caress her arm but she pulled back as though I had pricked her.

'I am sorry, but it pains a lot,' she said, as she pulled me closer and began weeping in my chest.

'Don't worry, sweetheart. I promise that nobody will ever hurt you again in the future,' I said, stroking her hair.

24

Basic Human Rights

'I thought the message was pretty clear to you: DO NOT COME HERE UNLESS YOU HAVE A WARRANT!' Neil told Inspector KK and his crony, Badri Prasad, both of whom stood at the Olympus Bar in the Grand Stage area of the club. Doesn't this country understand basic human rights?'

Both the policemen were dressed in civilian clothing, a far cry from the khaki uniform they had donned during their first visit to Kapital.

'I would be annoyed at meeting myself again and again too,' said KK, clad in a white shirt and jeans. 'But trust me, Mr Ramamurthy, we are here purely on an urge to experience the good life. You know what I mean. We want to party where the rich folk party. Drink the same fine liquor as them. Isn't that right, Badri?' KK threw the baton at his subordinate.

Badri, who was sipping on an iced mango margarita through a straw, nodded his head vigorously up and down to show that he was absolutely satisfied with whatever his boss just said.

'That's a load of bullsh—' Neil raged.

'What a pleasant surprise, inspector!' Sameera swooped in, having just arrived at the scene. She fixed her gaze at KK, oblivious to Badri's presence, an omission he did not mind in the least. He had a fruit cocktail to finish after all.

'Good to see you too, Miss Kapoor. I see that you wasted no time in re-opening the club!' jibed KK

'Work is worship in *my* line of work, Inspector!' Sameera wasn't subtle in handing the jibe back.

'Even then, it feels awfully early to open the nightclub again, especially when somebody died right here just a week ago,' said KK with a smile, not perturbed by the exchange of shielded insults.

'It is what Pari would have wanted for Kapital. She was really invested in the workings and promotions of the club,' said Sameera, her tone dropping its former sarcasm in exchange for candour.

As the music grew louder, the young drunk party-goers on the dance floor peeled away their inhibitions, if any. KK said something but it drowned in the noise.

'Enjoy your evening, gentlemen!' Sameera quipped to the policemen in her shrill voice, but she wasn't sure whether or not her words reached KK. Nevertheless, she pulled Neil aside, and both of them disappeared from the scene.

'If you are done with your drink, maybe we can focus on work,' said KK to Badri, whose drink was long over but he was still trying to retrieve the residual syrup from the glass by obscenely sucking through the straw.

'Give me two more minutes please, boss,' said Badri, but a stern look from his superior made him keep the glass down at the bar table instantly.

'Good!' said KK.

'So, what is our plan of action?' asked Badri.

'I need to lurk around in this area for some time and look for something,' said KK.

'Look for what, boss?' asked Badri.

'I don't know yet. But I will know once I come across it,' said KK cryptically.

'So, what should we do next? Where shall we begin?' asked Badri.

KK scanned the entirety of the club from his position by the Olympus Bar. It was at full capacity that night. He tried to create a mental image of the area from the time when he first came there. It was completely empty then. Empty and well-lit. He tried to recall the exact details of the layout. His mental pencil began drawing a diagram with all the salient features. The entry and exit doors. The emergency escape routes. The washrooms. The small office that was hidden behind a false wall. Everything popped out on a hologram in his mind. But there was something that was still evading him. What was it? He tried to focus his mind amidst the deafening music of the club, but he kept getting distracted. Why was his brain bringing school memories from his childhood all of a sudden?

'Focus, KK. Focus,' he told himself.

But there it was again, memories from his school days. Okay, he would see these through and then try to work on the case. He thought of the time when there was the annual day function in the school auditorium. Since he was no good at acting or dancing or singing, he was the default member of the Audio-Visual (AV) team, an unenviable one-man department. Apart from adjusting the volume of the microphones, his duties included climbing over the fake ceiling of the stage and replacing the broken bulbs of studio lights. What was the point of this specific memory? Why bring it up now? Unless . . . EUREKA! There had to be a floor above this which would be used for light installation. But how do you get there? The elevator showed a total of twenty floors and Kapital was on the twentieth floor.

'Let's get down to work, KK.'

KK saw a server walking around with a tray of onion rings when the proverbial light bulb switched on in his mind. There was only one area on this floor that he hadn't looked around—the kitchen. And it would make sense to keep access to the hidden floor through the kitchen; any onsite maintenance could be carried out without disturbing the nightclub. That was the only plausible explanation!

'Badri, listen to me,' he said to his junior who had been left smitten by the free-flowing dance moves of two short-skirted women.

'Yes, boss!' said Badri, his eyes still focusing on the two girls.

'I am going to the kitchen. You stay here,' said KK.

'Okay, boss. You go. I'll stay here,' said Badri, without moving his eyes.

'Stay put, and if anybody asks, tell them that I am in the washroom. I won't be long,' said KK.

'Understood boss,' said Badri, happy to stay put exactly where he was. Ah! The perks of the job.

KK retrieved an ID card from his pocket and wore its lanyard around his neck. It was a neat trick that he had learnt when he was a rookie cop. Nobody ever stopped a person with an ID card. KK made his way towards the kitchen. It was easy to spot. He just had to follow any random waiter carrying an empty tray.

KK entered the kitchen and found it exactly how he had expected it. There were people in white uniforms and headgear performing all sorts of tasks. Cleaning, chopping, boiling, frying and everything else. A rather short man, whose uniform seemed to be of richer material than the others was barking orders at everybody else. On seeing the intruder in his kitchen, he stopped speaking.

'Yes? Have you lost your way, mister?'

'Me? No! I am here to fix the broken studio light,' said KK, gently holding his ID card to seem legit.

'To fix the studio light at this time? it is almost 10 p.m.,' said the chef, checking his watch.

'Miss Kapoor told my boss that it was urgent. A light is malfunctioning on the dance floor, and it needs to be fixed as soon as possible,' said KK.

'Strange. I haven't received any such information,' said the chef.

'I don't know about the chain of communication at this place. All I know is that a malfunctioning piece of equipment has to be fixed on a priority basis, especially in light of the recent incident,' said KK and that was it. 'In the light of the recent incident' was the golden phrase KK needed to be given access to the forbidden area.

The chef nodded, 'Follow me.'

KK trod on the heels of the chef till he took him to the absolute dead end of the kitchen. The chef opened a small almirah-like door on his right. It was too dark to see inside. KK switched on his phone's flashlight and discovered a rusty steel ladder placed against the wall.

'Good luck climbing this rattling old thing,' said the chef as he held the door open for KK.

'I am used to it. It is an everyday thing for me,' said KK cooly, masking the sudden rush of anxiety as he climbed the first step.

The chef did not wait for a single second before shutting the door and leaving KK all by himself in claustrophobic darkness.

'Okay, KK! You got this buddy,' KK told himself as he tucked his phone in his shirt's chest pocket with its flash turned on and the video camera recording.

The passageway was no bigger than the size of an elevator. The light from his phone only illuminated the current area in front of him. There was complete darkness above and below him. As KK made his way up, so did his anxiety.

'Few more steps only! Come on, KK! You can conquer anything that you set your mind to,' he told himself, recalling a one-liner from a self-help book that he had read many years ago.

Three more steps and KK reached where he wanted to go—the floor above the false ceiling. It was a vast expanse of wooden ground spread directly above Kapital but only four feet in height with no room to stand up. KK crouched on all fours and began crawling towards where the music was coming from. 'I am crossing the kitchen from above,' he told himself out loud.

The floor was dusty and covered in small stones that pinched KK's palms. But as he crawled further and further, he realized that he wasn't alone on the false floor. A colony of rats moved around, squeaking and scurrying freely on the wooden log tiles. The tiny little pellets were not stones but rat-shit, and his hands and favourite trousers were now covered in it. He was certain that his laundry lady would raise a serious objection but that was a problem for later. He gasped at that thought when he felt the floor below him vibrating. As he crawled a little further, the vibrations grew stronger. He was directly above the club's dance floor. The area in front of it had nuts and bolts fixtures attached to the floor.

'This should be where those shiny lights are fixed,' he wondered out loud.

'Now where is the exact location of that bloody light which fell on Pari Chadha?'

He stopped crawling and sat up straight on his knees. He removed the phone from his shirt pocket and held it. The phone flashlight gave him a better view as he scanned the area before him.

'That side is more crowded with light fixtures than the others. That should be right above the DJ stage, and Pari happened to be somewhere near that.'

A rush of adrenaline replaced the erstwhile anxiety in his body as his limbs moved in the said direction at a brisk pace. One light fixture seemed cleaner and shinier than the others. The wooden floor plank underneath it was of a different shade than the ones surrounding it.

'Okay so, this is where they must have installed the new light and the new wooden log tile. I am above the exact spot where it happened. Bingo!' he told himself.

But KK's euphoria was short-lived. He felt a pair of hands grab him by the ankles and yank him. He came crashing to the floor, his phone slipping out of his grasp and smashing onto the planks below him.

Ambushed, agitated and anxious, there was only one thought on his mind: *Was this the end?*

25

An Unnecessary Disaster

'KK, if the next words from your mouth aren't "sorry sir", then I promise that this is your last day on the force,' a furious Jaiswal spat out, sporting an untucked and unironed shirt over trousers and chappals, and an inglorious pair of dark circles under his eyes.

'Sorry, sir!' said KK, his head hung down in shame.

It was around 11 p.m., and the party of seven were standing in the lobby of The Grand Majestic Hotel. The representatives from the police included KK and Badri obviously, and KK's boss, Jaiswal, who had been summoned by Sameera at this ungodly hour. Jaiswal, who had gone to bed at 9 p.m. in order to be fresh for his 4:30 a.m. golf session with his buddies, wasn't pleased to find himself in the middle of the conundrum that KK had created.

Team Kapital included Sameera, Neil, Gyan Singh, who had caught KK red-handed as he was sneaking onto the false floor and Chef Alex, who was the one who had alerted Sameera about the presence of 'a certain light technician with suspect motives'.

'If he actually was a light technician, why wasn't he carrying a tool kit with himself? That made me very suspicious,' Chef Alex had repeatedly said this out loud to anyone who would listen.

'This behaviour is just not acceptable, CP Jaiswal,' said Sameera. 'Cops like Kiran Kumar are a blot on the entire police force. This is pure harassment of common people like us.'

'I apologize on behalf of my officer, ma'am,' said Jaiswal, who desperately wanted to be back home and be golf-ready tomorrow.

'An apology is not enough,' said Neil. 'We are going to sue the entire police department for unlawful spying on common citizens.'

'Oh God!' muttered Jaiswal under his breath before he made himself loud enough for the benefit of the entire group. 'Mr Ramamurthy, it was a mistake, a genuine mistake from my officer. I will make sure that it doesn't happen again.'

'If it were the United States, this officer would already be off the force,' said Neil, his nostrils flaring. 'I demand a similar action over here.'

'I am sorry, sir. But that is not possible,' said Jaiswal, sweating profusely from every body part capable of sweating. 'I agree that it is an act of indiscipline and an appropriate action will be taken against him. But I can't kick him off the force.'

KK, standing behind Jaiswal with a lowered head, developed a new-found respect for his senior for sticking by him in this situation. Meanwhile, Badri, still a little buzzed from the iced-mango margarita, stood quietly in stand-at-ease to avoid drawing any attention to himself.

'Okay then, expect a lawsuit against the entire Delhi police force for harassment tomorrow morning,' said Neil, a veteran consumer of many American law TV shows.

'That's correct,' said Sameera, holding her phone in her hands. 'I am dialling Hiranandani, my lawyer right away.'

'KK, you are suspended without pay for six months,' said Jaiswal without missing a beat. 'You will need to deposit your department-issued badge and weapon in the office tomorrow.'

'But sir . . .' KK tried to protest.

'No buts, KK. My decision is final,' said Jaiswal, looking at his watch, hoping to close this and get back to bed. 'Badri, you are suspended too.'

KK realized that there was no point in arguing, especially with a fuming audience in front of them. It wasn't his boss' fault. He tried his best to stand up for him, but it wasn't meant to be tonight.

26

A Million Bucks

'The ring looks perfect on your finger, my dear!' said Neil's Mom, a lady in her early sixties with her thick grey hair tied neatly in a bun. A pair of reading glasses sat comfortably at the tip of her nose.

'Thank you, Aunty,' replied a blushing Sameera, as she showcased the sparkling piece of rock to her future mother-in-law through the iPad.

'Don't call me 'aunty!' You should call me "Mom" now, dear,' said Neil's Mom.

'Maa, come on! Don't put so much pressure on her already,' quipped Neil, coming to the rescue of his brand-new fiancé.

'What is wrong with calling me "Mom?"' His mother asked melodramatically, giving those Indian soap opera ladies a run for their money.

'There is nothing wrong, Maa, but,' Neil began to explain. 'It gets overwhelming . . .'

'Shut up, Neil! It is not overwhelming,' said Sameera, cutting Neil in between.

'It is a pleasure to address your mother as "Mom", which she now technically is. Isn't that correct, Mom?'

'You are right, my dear,' said Neil's Mom, looking happier than a bumper lottery winner. 'Neil, consider yourself an extremely lucky man to have such a sensible woman in your life.'

'Not just one, Mom,' said Sameera, smirking at Neil. 'He has two sensible women in his life. His Mom and his fiancé.'

'Neil, marry this woman already,' commanded his mother through the screen.

'I will, Maa!' said Neil, pretending to be flustered. 'But first can you both tone down on this fresh mother-in-law/daughter-in-law bonding? It is too much to take on!'

'Ah! Ever so dramatic, Neil!' taunted his Mom. 'Stop with your theatrics.'

'Oh, Mom! Tell me about it,' Sameera joined in at burning her fiancé.

'Okay, guys! So, I am going to take a little walk and get some fresh air while both of you continue your camaraderie,' said Neil, getting up from the lounge chair.

'Oh, honey! We were just joking,' called out Sameera, making a cute puppy face. 'Don't go!'

'Babe, I need some fresh air,' said Neil, moving out of his mother's vision to signal that he was stepping out for a smoke.

Before Sameera could say anything, Neil's Mom spoke. 'Sameera dear, let him go. My son wants to go and smoke a cigarette.'

'But Maa! How did you?' said a bewildered Neil.

'I am your mother, dear,' she said. 'I carried you inside me for over nine months. I know you more than you know yourself.'

'Fine,' said a deflated and defeated Neil. 'I'll be back in a bit, the both of you carry on!'

'Yes. Take your time, son,' she said and brought her attention back to Sameera. 'Dear, I have some ideas for your wedding!'

'Absolutely, Mom! I would love to hear them!' said Sameera with a bright glow on her face.

Twenty minutes later, Sameera was greeted by a thick cloud of cigarette smoke as she opened the bathroom door of the master bedroom. She found Neil sitting neck-deep in a bubbly water-filled bathtub, a freshly lit cigarette in his hand, and several extinguished buds floating in a glass resting at the edge of the tub.

'Well, well!' said Sameera. 'Mr Ramamurthy in his natural habitat!'

'This is my version of therapy,' replied Neil, taking in a deep relaxing puff. 'Especially after that intense ganging up that happened against me!'

'Come on! It wasn't that bad,' snorted Sameera. 'We were just pulling your leg.'

Neil smiled fondly, 'I'm kidding, sweetheart. But it was cute to see you bonding with my mother. You guys got along like a house on fire.'

'Your Mom is the sweetest,' said Sameera ecstatically. 'I love her already!'

'That was evident,' said Neil, smiling before taking in another puff. 'I wish I had introduced both of you sooner.'

'I know, right!' gushed Sameera. 'She wants us to have a grand wedding in Boston. And when I told her that I wanted a wedding in Delhi as well, she got even more excited. She said that we should have wedding ceremonies across continents. One each in India and Boston. How crazy is that?'

'It is very crazy indeed,' agreed Neil as he reached the fag end of his cigarette. 'Do you know what is even crazier?'

'What?' asked Sameera.

'Your unique ability to connect with anybody and make them feel special,' said Neil, throwing the bud in the glass.

'Shut up! Stop teasing me,' said Sameera.

'No, I am serious, darling,' said Neil. 'My purpose of vanishing into the bathroom was to give you guys some space. It is very important for me that Maa and you develop a good organic relationship. Both of you are the only family that I have.'

'And you both, mine,' said Sameera, feeling engulfed in emotions.

'And trust me,' continued Neil, not breaking eye contact with his fiancé. 'I've never seen her open up so easily with anybody else, Sam, you can make people feel like a million bucks!'

'I don't know what to say, Neil! That was so sweet,' said Sameera, almost teary-eyed.

'What's more to say? Come on, join me in the tub. There's room for two!' Neil winked at her.

'Yes, sir!' said Sameera as she removed her heels.

It was day seven of the suspension. KK used the key hidden under the doormat to enter his apartment for the first time since the morning. It was a 2BHK. Small but sufficient for him. He used one bedroom for himself, while the other, originally designated for his future kids, had now been converted into a storeroom of sorts. One half of the bed supported an entire fort made of neatly stacked cardboard carton boxes. Some of the boxes had 'Nafisa' written on them with a red permanent marker. The other half of the bed had become a dumping ground for a wide spectrum of clothes: ironed, washed but not ironed, worn once but can be used again, need to be washed, and so on. As KK made his way towards the kitchen, he passed an array of photo frames hung on the wall. The first frame had him, the groom with a head full of hair, and his bride smiling shyly at the camera at their wedding reception. In the second frame, he and his bride posed as if they were trying to touch the tip of the Taj Mahal. The third had the both of them peddling away gleefully on a boat in a lake. All the photographs were now accumulating dust.

The kitchen too was not an image of organized living. Plates upon plates had made a filthy mountain in the sink. The dustbin overflowed with empty Swiggy and Zomato packets and had probably become a breeding ground for insects. KK opened the fridge and retrieved himself a half-full jar of peanut butter and a bread loaf that was way past its date of expiry. When he was halfway through his sandwich, the bell to his apartment rang and startled him.

Who could be there at this time? He checked his phone in case he had placed an online food delivery order and forgotten about it, which was a very real possibility. Nothing on any of the apps. KK scrapped the crumbs from his trousers and got up to get the door. Nobody was standing outside. Must be a prank by those rascal neighbourhood kids. One of these days he would catch them red-handed and teach them a lesson. KK shut the door and came back to finish his meal when the bell rang for the second time. These kids better brace themselves for the calamity that they had invited on themselves! He rushed towards the door and flung it open only to find nobody there again.

He looked sideways at the passageway. Nobody. He almost shut the door when he noticed a small, battered shoebox wrapped in brown packaging tape on the floor. He picked it up and brought it inside to the dining table.

He cut through the tape with the peanut butter-laden table knife and separated the lid from the rest of the box. A small solitary slip of paper rested on bundles of 500-rupee notes. It simply read: 'Call the number given below.'

Was this a bribe? Else, there was no reason for such a windfall amount to arrive at a policeman's doorstep, unsolicited. KK had been an honest cop so far in his career. But how had that turned out for him? Whatever it is that the person on the other end of the phone wanted, he would give it serious consideration.

'Hello?' asked KK after dialling the given digits. 'Who is this?'

'I knew you would not disappoint me, Inspector Kiran Kumar,' said Bunty Gulati from the other end.

'What do you want? What is the meaning of all this cash? Is this a bribe?' asked KK, his nostrils flaring. He had to stay in character as an honest policeman till the time he didn't have all the information.

'A bribe?' scoffed Bunty. 'This is gratitude, inspector.'

'Gratitude for what?' asked KK, genuinely surprised.

'For your effort to bring down a common enemy,' said Bunty from the other end.

'What are you talking about?' asked KK, but he figured the answer out himself before Bunty had a chance to talk. 'You sent me that package at the Police Station! Didn't you?'

'You are smart, Inspector Kiran,' said Bunty with a villainous laugh. 'Yes, it was I who sent you evidence that the spotlight at Kapital had been tampered with!'

'And what about this money?' asked KK. 'I cannot help you with anything illegal.'

'Illegal? There is nothing illegal about this inspector,' said Bunty, sounding agitated from the other end. 'All I want is justice.'

'Justice? For whom?' asked KK. 'Who are you? Are you a relative of Pari Chadha?'

'My name is Bunty Gulati,' said Bunty. 'I was wronged by that wretched woman, Sameera Kapoor. If justice had been served earlier then that poor girl, Pari, would have been alive today. I want Sameera Kapoor behind bars before somebody else becomes a victim.'

'What did Sameera Kapoor do to you?' asked KK, amused at the turn of events while his half-eaten sandwich lay in front of him. His appetite was being filled by something far more interesting.

'I'll fill you in with all the details if you agree to help me, Inspector,' said Bunty. As an incentive, I have sent you five lakh rupees. You will get five lakh more on the completion of the job.'

'Mr Gulati, as I already mentioned to you, I cannot do anything ille- . . .' said KK before Bunty interjected him.

'Yes yes, you already mentioned your aversion to anything illegal,' said Bunty.

'But I am not asking you to do anything illegal at all. I will provide you with the information that will help bring down Sameera Kapoor and her American fiancé and also re-instate you back in the police force before your six-month suspension period lapses.'

'Then why the bribe?' asked KK, for whom getting his badge back was incentive enough.

'In our line of work, we believe in the dignity of labour, Inspector,' said Bunty. 'Consider it as a small token of gratitude and appreciation.'

'Mr Gulati, I'll admit that your proposition looks enticing to me,' said KK. 'But how do I know for sure that I am not being taken for a ride? What is the legitimacy of your information?'

'Relax, inspector,' said Bunty with a devilish calmness to him. 'You will have to trust me on this. Let us just say that I have somebody on the inside leaking information to me.'

'Somebody on the inside? Who?' asked KK.

'Don't ask questions and you will be told no lies, Inspector Kiran,' said Bunty. 'I can't reveal my source until the job is done.'

KK did not say anything. His mind began playing the various ways the Rs 10,00,000 could impact his life. He thought of the foreign trips that he had enviously watched his colleagues take on Instagram, while he couldn't gather sufficient funds for a paltry Goa trip. He thought of the hair transplant surgery that he had been delaying for two years. Also, his father's regular dialysis treatment! That was chipping away his savings faster than the speed of light. KK was due a life upgrade, and here was fate, handing one right up at his doorstep.

'Hello? Are you there, Inspector Kiran Kumar?' asked Bunty, after no no response from KK.

'I am in,' said KK. 'I'll do it!'

'That is awesome,' gushed Bunty. 'My intuition was correct. I could count on you. Let me call you tomorrow around the same time and discuss the plan. We execute in three days.'

'Perfect,' said KK. 'But one last thing?'

'What is it?' asked Bunty.

'Call me KK!'

27

Shitstorm

The phone seemingly rang with the ferocity of an airplane engine. Sameera snuck one hand out of her duvet and declined the call. It rang again and received the same fate.

'Who is this moron trying to reach you this early in this morning?' asked Neil, half-annoyed-half-asleep as he snuggled his arms around Sameera and made her the little spoon.

'God knows! Whatever it is, I can deal with it later,' said Sameera, a combination of sleepy and annoyed herself.

The blissful silence was back on in the bedroom. Only the white noise of the air-con running in the background and the slow gentle snores of two lovers who had tired each other out last night. When the phone rang for the third time, Sameera's dormant volcano erupted. She grabbed it in anger and yelled at the caller.

'Do you have any idea what time it is?'

But as soon as she heard what the caller on the other end had to say, her anger took a backseat. After hanging up, she stood straight up on her feet, wide awake. The idea of getting back into the cozy bed with her fiancé stopped being tempting.

'Who was it, Sam?" asked Neil from the bed.

'Gyan Singh.'

'What did he want at this time?' asked Neil, rubbing his eyes.

'He asked me to switch the TV on to a news channel,' replied Sameera, trying to locate the remote on the side table.

'What? Is he bonkers? The news channel at this time?' replied Neil, hoping to get a reaction out from Sameera, but when she didn't respond at all, he sat up straight in the bed, sensing something was horribly wrong.

'Sweetheart, what is it? Why does Gyan Singh want us to switch on to a news channel?' he asked, meanwhile Sameera had already gotten hold of the TV remote. She switched it on and killed the suspense.

'This is Sushil Pandey from News 69 live from the studio. We have breaking news for you,' said a pony-tailed reporter, wearing a parrot green three-piece suit, his screechy voice grating at their ears. 'Kapital, Delhi's newest and most happening place to party, situated in

The Grand Majestic Hotel, has been in the news for all the wrong reasons lately. Just to refresh your memory, on its opening day, party-goers were greeted with a fire breakout in the club. Even though there were no casualties, it was enough to scare a few of its would-be patrons.'

The screen transitioned to show a hospital bed and a man lying on it, covered in bandages on his head, arms and legs. As the camera closed up on him, Neil and Sameera realized that the man in the bandages was a dear foe from their recent past.

'When things were coming back to normal, Bunty Gulati, a Delhi resident who made the mistake of celebrating his twenty-fifth birthday at Kapital, was beaten up black-and-blue by the members of Kapital's staff.'

'What is this rascal doing here!' said Neil out aloud.

'This is a load of BS!' gasped Sameera.

'Let us hear what this low life has to say for himself,' Neil said, watching as Bunty began talking on the screen.

'It was the eve of my twenty-fifth birthday,' began Bunty, pacing his voice at a snail's speed as he squeezed a few crocodile tears from his eyes. 'My friends ordered drinks at the bar. Sameera Kapoor was standing next to us. At that time, we didn't know that she was the owner of the club and the hotel. For some reason, she started hurling abuses at us. We realized that she was drunk, so we didn't try to engage her. We just wanted to get our drinks and get back to the dance floor. But Miss Kapoor was relentless. She said some really nasty things to us. We asked her politely to let us party in peace. The next thing we knew she called her boyfriend, a dude with an American accent, and some bouncers to beat us up. Ouch, it pains even now!'

'Ha ha ha!' said Sameera slowly clapping her hands. 'If this isn't the performance of the century, I don't know what it is! Is the Oscars committee watching this?'

'This guy has some balls!' said Neil, as the pony-tailed TV anchor came back on screen.

'Let us hear the first-hand account of the incident from Mr Bunty's friends, who were also manhandled by the club security but were lucky enough to make it out on their two feet.'

The camera panned at a group of four boys, all of them bruised and bandaged at various parts of their bodies. It was the Gucci Gang, who had chosen to shed their high-street attire for plain insipid kurta-pyjamas. One by one the four of them narrated their nightmarish ordeal at Kapital. At the end of their collective sob stories, they clasped their hands together in unison and said, 'Boycott Kapital!'

#BoycottKapital appeared below the screen just in time when Sameera shut the television off.

'Can you believe these guys? This is slander! This is defamation!' Neil was fuming.

'Babe, let's get ready and go downstairs. It is time to lawyer up!' said Sameera coolly. 'These people have messed with the wrong person.'

'What do you mean he is on vacation? I need him right now! Tell him to contact me A-S-A-P!' said Sameera, completely riled up as she and Neil stepped out of the elevator into the hotel lobby.

Sameera had changed into her battle attire—a light grey pantsuit with an off-white shirt while Neil, true to his style wore a heavy-weight round-neck tee with jeans.

'What was that about? Who is on a vacation?' enquired Neil.

'Hiranandani, my lawyer,' snorted Sameera.

'Oh no,' said Neil, patting her on the back. 'What is our next plan of action?'

'I don't know, Neil,' said Sameera, flustered. 'I literally just told Hiranandani's secretary to make his ass fly back to Delhi immediately. I am so bloody annoyed. I want to punch something!'

'Calm down, take a deep breath,' said Neil, trying not to become his fiancé's accidental punching bag. Sameera did as she was told and within a few seconds, her anger dropped down by a few notches.

'Babe,' said Neil. 'I fail to understand why Bunty and his scum gang are creating this drama and theatrics months after the incident happened? I mean why bring it up now?'

'Strike when the iron is hot,' said Sameera, like a seasoned war general. 'They are capitalizing on the Pari incident.'

But before she could elaborate, the usually calm and stoical Gyan Singh arrived huffing and puffing on the scene.

'Boss Madam, you need to come with me,' said Gyan Singh, trying to gather his breath. 'I have to show you something!'

'What's the matter, Gyan Singh? Where do you want me to come?' asked Sameera, her heart jumping in her mouth. If Gyan Singh had lost his composure, then it meant that shit had indeed hit the fan.

'To the security room, Boss Madam. Right away,' said Gyan Singh.

The security room was a misnomer for the surveillance room, which was tucked behind the reception of the hotel lobby. Back in the day, when The Grand Majestic Hotel had just begun its operations, the security room was the place where all the security personnel came to take a break between their shifts. As the hotel grew in scale and magnitude, the actual security room moved outside of the main premises, and the newly vacated room became home to state-of-the-art surveillance equipment and technology. The high-definition cameras kept track of all the events happening in the hotel and displayed a live feed on the hi-resolution monitors which covered three out of four walls of the room.

As soon as Sameera entered the room along with Neil and Gyan Singh, two men in security uniforms stood up from their chairs and saluted their boss. Sameera gave them a nod, an acknowledgement of their salute.

'Boss Madam, look here, outside the hotel,' said Gyan Singh, pointing at a monitor screen on the left wall.

Sameera looked at the screen and exclaimed, 'Holy fuck! What is all that?'

Outside the gates of The Grand Majestic Hotel, a fleet of media vans, with satellite antennas and their respective news channel's logos, had parked themselves. A gaggle of news reporters were speaking into the camera with The Grand Majestic Hotel in the background.

'This is ridiculous! A media shitstorm because of a measly club brawl! I can't believe it!' exclaimed Neil, his eyes fixated on the screen.

'This is Bunty's doing. People get beaten up every single day of the year in Delhi. No big deal about it,' said Sameera, echoing her fiancé's views.

A mobile phone rang. The ringtone was strange and yet oddly familiar. Gyan Singh answered the call on his ancient Nokia as everybody looked on. He listened to what the caller had to say before he relayed it to his employer.

'This reporting is not about that birthday party, Boss Madam,' Gyan Singh informed her. 'This seems like something else altogether.'

Sameera looked at him with blank eyes. *What is happening?*

'The media people are talking about Pari Chadha's death. They are calling it a murder,' said Gyan Singh with the graveness of a doctor informing a toddler's parents that their child has terminal cancer.

'Bullshit! Totally ridiculous,' Neil said punching the air.

'Put on a news channel,' Sameera said quietly, and when no immediate action was taken, she presented a more assertive demonstration of her command, lest anybody think it was a request. 'Goddamnit! Put on a bloody news channel!'

The outburst was enough to rattle the security personnel standing directly in front of her. He pressed some keys in nervous haste and five seconds later, News 69 was playing on the front monitor. The ponytailed anchor with the gratingly screechy voice graced the screen. He had changed into an eye-stinging orange suit, and this time, instead of the studio, the battlefield was as close to home as it could get.

'I am standing outside The Grand Majestic Hotel in New Delhi. Yes, it is the same hotel that houses the

infamous club, Kapital, where we told you in our early
morning broadcast that Bunty Gulati was beaten up.
A few days ago, Pari Chadha, a popular social media
influencer, lost her life due to a studio light falling on
her head. Now, another disturbing detail has come to
our knowledge. Earlier this incident was brushed off
as an accident, but there is more to it than meets the
eye. We have Inspector KK from Delhi Police who will
elaborate.'

The security room watch-party collectively grew
uneasy as they saw Inspector KK, another recent foe
who was supposed to be serving his suspension period,
appear on the screen in his police uniform and a pair
of aviator sunglasses.

'Looks like every member of the Anti-Kapital club
is gathered here today,' muttered Sameera under her
breath.

'The case is currently under investigation, and I
won't be able to reveal key information,' said KK as
he went on to reveal every bit of information possible
on national television. 'Our investigating team has
discovered that Sameera Kapoor has taken a massive
loan against her properties. The exact amount of the
loan is uncertain right now, but it is at least to the
tune of twenty crore rupees, if not more. After the
pandemic, The Grand Majestic Hotel has been under
tremendous debt after facing terrible losses. It is
suspected that Sameera Kapoor figured a way to get
out of this financial mess by rashly reopening Kapital,

a club that had been shut since the death of her mother. Sameera took out hefty insurance policies on her club and deliberately installed sub-standard equipment, which was bound to get her insurance claims from the company.'

There was a strategic pause in KK's monologue for the audience to digest in the shocking information. He cleared his throat and continued.

'The reason that Pari Chadha is dead today is because Sameera Kapoor chose to install equipment that would endanger lives at her club while she receives a handsome payout. This is not only a case of occupational negligence but also murder!'

Neil looked at Sameera, but he couldn't gauge her reaction. She stood still in front of the monitor, soaking in every single word spoken against her. The tension in the room was palpable.

'Neil, do you know why the news channel started with the whole Bunty Gulati episode in the early morning broadcast?' asked Sameera when she finally spoke.

'I literally have no fucking idea about what is going on!' admitted Neil.

'It was to warm the public opinion up against me. The main weapon in the arsenal was always supposed to be the Pari Chadha story,' said Sameera.

'Holy shit! This is a bloody conspiracy!' exclaimed Neil, as he saw a tall lanky man appear on the screen who looked vaguely familiar.

'Sam, isn't this the insurance guy who came to the club after the opening day fire?' asked Neil, having a lightbulb moment.

'He is! Puneet Saxena from NSM Insurance!' said Sameera, clenching her fist.

'Yes, it is true that Miss Kapoor was expecting a huge insurance payout for her club, but the company could not substantiate her claims at that time,' said Puneet Saxena to the reporter.

Gyan Singh's phone rang for the second time in the Security Room, causing everybody to look to him for more updates. After the call was done, he quietly said, 'Boss Madam, the police are on the hotel premises, and they are looking for you. It is best if you stay in the security room. I shall tell them that you are not on the property currently.'

'No, you will do no such thing,' instructed Sameera. 'I will go and talk to them. This bogus campaign is an attempt to malign my image. I will clear this on my own.'

KK, in his aviators, and Badri, standing proudly with his lathi, were waiting in the lobby, as half a dozen policemen stood behind them.

'Officers, there has been a huge misunderstanding,' said Sameera, entering the scene with her own entourage consisting of Neil, Gyan Singh and a few hotel security guards. But before she could finish her sentence, KK shoved a piece of paper in her face.

'We have a warrant for your arrest, Sameera Kapoor,' KK said in a clear calm voice.

'Arrest warrant? Are you guys fucking joking?' said Neil, who did not expect that the morning would come to this. 'Weren't you and your sidekick on suspension?'

'Sir, we request you not to use such foul language with an officer of the law,' said KK, wielding a weird combo of power and tranquillity. 'Effective today, we have been reinstated into the police department.'

'What a load of BS,' said Neil, his emotions all riled up. 'Just because some lowlife gives a TV interview about being beaten up, it doesn't give you the right to arrest an innocent woman. Bloody morons, all of you!'

KK remained unfazed by Neil's comments. A pair of female officers appeared from the group of cops. One of them slapped a handcuff on Sameera's wrist, except that it wouldn't close. The lady officer tried twice to click it shut but in vain. Seeing this, KK reached over, impulsively grabbing the handcuffs himself and closing them around Sameera's wrist using excessive force, an action that caused her to shriek out in pain.

'You bloody asshole! How dare you!' said Neil as he delivered a crisp slap on KK's face in full view of everybody in the hotel lobby, causing both KK's aviators and self-respect to fall on the recently mopped floor.

Generally, the range of vision from the twentieth floor is hazy, owing to the thick layer of smog that Delhi is perpetually enveloped in. But that particular morning, Chef Alex had a crystal-clear view of Sameera Kapoor and Neil Ramamurthy leaving the premises of The Grand Majestic Hotel in the police convoy.

28

Urine

The holding cell reeked of urine, vomit and other bodily fluids that Neil did not wish to identify. Except for one other person, the cell was completely empty. That other person had been sleeping soundly on the wooden bench in the far corner when Neil was inducted two hours ago. The sleeping man hadn't woken up ever since, which Neil was thankful for; he wasn't in any rush to meet his roomie.

Neil held the bars in his hands and shook them vigorously as he yelled for the millionth time, 'Let me out of here! I am an American citizen! You cannot hold me like this. I will sue you.'

The guard outside put his newspaper down and walked towards the bars to be face to face with Neil.

'Listen, you *akal ke dhakkan*! You must be an American citizen outside this jail. Right now, you are just a dimwit who assaulted a police officer. My free advice to you is—shut the fuck up and sit quietly in the corner or else I will beat the entire America out of your ass,' said the guard, and went back to his newspaper.

Neil took his advice and placed himself on a rickety old wooden bench.

'At least, can I get some water?' asked Neil nervously.

'Are you blind? Can't you see that pot and glass kept over there?' asked the guard referring to an earthen pot of water which Neil had earlier discovered to be a swimming pool for a bunch of flies, and the single steel glass which appeared to not have been washed in this century.

'Sir, the glass and the water don't seem to be hygienic. Can you please get me a bottle of mineral water?' asked Neil, his brashness long gone now.

The guard's eyes sparkled at the mention of the words 'mineral water.'

'Why, of course, sir! I will immediately send for some mineral water,' the guard said, standing up from his stool and bowing his head down to waist level.

'Would you want to accompany that with a seven-course meal from a five-star restaurant?'

Neil did not bother replying because a sensible conversation would be futile with this person. He sank back onto the bench with his feet folded up in a crossbow position. The floor was sticky from, what his best guess was, urine. He looked over at his roomie,

with whom introductions hadn't been exchanged
yet. He was still asleep even as a group of mosquitos
hovered above his head. He wondered how Sameera
was faring in her holding cell. He hadn't spoken to her
since the morning.

Gyan Singh held an iPad in his hands with the screen
facing the bars of the female holding cell, behind which
stood a frantic Sameera. The more she spoke, the more
pungent smell she inhaled from the disinfectant that
was recently used to mop the floor.

'Mr Hiranandani! You need to get my fiancé and
me out of this shithole ASAP,' said Sameera to the large
man gracing her iPad's screen, wearing a Hawaiian
shirt and holding an open coconut with a cocktail
umbrella. 'The police have taken Neil to a station in
Chandni Chowk, while I am locked up here in Saket.'

'Miss Kapoor, don't worry! I assure you that my team
is already working to get this sorted,' said Hiranandani.

'Your team is not good enough! I want you over
here in Delhi,' said Sameera, adamant and not taking
no for an answer.

'But Miss Kapoor, as I already told you, I am not in
the country. I have come abroad to celebrate my wife's
twenty-third birthday,' said Hiranandani pointing the
camera towards a busty woman in a two-piece bikini
lying on a beach bed with a piña colada by her side.

Sameera remembered liking Hiranandani's pictures from his fourth wedding on Instagram a couple of months ago.

'Mr Hiranandani, I don't care. Move heaven and earth if you have to but sort this issue out for me. Get me the bail,' Sameera told him.

'Don't worry, Miss Kapoor. Currently, as it is Independence Day weekend, the district magistrate is not available. But my team is working a way out,' said Hiranandani.

'Give me results, Mr Hiranandani,' demanded Sameera.

Hiranandani said something but it was gibberish. There was a lag in the internet connection. His screen froze and after multiple seconds of waiting, Sameera killed the video chat. Gyan Singh folded the iPad back into its cover. Sameera sat down on the long stool and buried her head in her palms. She was the only person in the holding cell. The guards outside had been accommodating in her request for home-supplied food and water, and free access to her PA, Gyan Singh. All for a small undocumented fee, of course.

'What are your orders, Boss Madam?' asked Gyan Singh.

'I literally have no idea, Gyan Singh,' Sameera confessed. 'One moment everything was normal, and then all of a sudden the sky fell on my head.'

'Boss Madam, you will get through this. I am certain of it.'

'I can't even imagine what poor Neil is going through being holed up in an Indian jail like this.'

'He must be fine. Don't worry about him, Boss Madam. Let us first focus on how to get you out. You cannot help him while you yourself are here,' Gyan Singh said, radiating a wise monk energy.

'Maybe, I can,' said Sameera, having a sudden brainwave. 'Gyan Singh, first, I need you to find a contact in the American Embassy. Maybe we can find somebody who can help Neil.'

'Done,' said Gyan Singh. 'I shall get on it straight away. Anything else?'

'Yes, go find me a more competent lawyer who can arrange for me to get out of here while I still have my sanity with me!' said Sameera, stomping her foot on the ground.

'Consider it done, Boss Madam.'

'Boss, you should try some too! This is just out of the world,' said Badri as he pushed a plate of chholey-bhaturey in front of KK.

'No, thanks. I am not hungry,' said KK, nudging the plate back to his junior. He was busy dialing a number that had gone unanswered for the eleventh time in a row now. 'Where the hell are you, Bunty?' he muttered under his breath.

'Who is Bunty, boss?' asked Badri.

'Nobody,' said KK. 'Umm, he's an old informant of mine.'

'All right, you can call him later,' said Badri. 'This is our first day being back on the job. We should celebrate. These bhaturas are from the famous Ram Halwai shop in Rajouri,'

'I am good, thank you,' said KK, who was still distracted by his phone.

'All right then,' said Badri, putting the crisp bhatura on his own plate. 'Just so you know, you perhaps are the only person in this world who has refused to eat these yummy bhaturas. Hats off to your willpower, I must say.'

'Thanks,' said KK, stoically.

'What's up, boss? Why so chatty today?' asked a concerned Badri. 'We caught those rich bastards. You should be celebrating.'

'It's nothing, Badri,' said KK.

'Come on, it must be something that is bothering you,' said Badri, being the rare subordinate to treat his boss as a friend.

'There are still missing bits to the case,' said KK. 'I am not able to put a finger to it yet.'

'Like what?'

'I don't know yet,' said KK, 'What if the information through my informant was nothing but a set-up? What if we got all this wrong?'

'As in we got the Kapital case wrong? Come on, boss!' said Badri, standing up at the preposterous suggestion. 'We got them almost dead to rights. Sameera Kapoor should be in jail! She endangered the lives of so many people only for an insurance payout. A clear slam dunk if you ask me.'

'Yes, you are right,' said KK after thinking for a while. 'Pass me that chholey-bhaturey.'

Badri had never felt happier when sharing food.

The lady constable shone a bright torchlight on Sameera's face through the darkness. It was late at night and all the lights of the holding cell were switched off. Sameera hadn't slept a wink. She lay down on the bench and closed her eyes but the constant paranoia of being stuck in a place like this had kept her wide awake.

'Are you Sameera Kapoor?' the lady constable asked, the torch pointed right at Sameera's eyes.

'Yes, I am,' said Sameera putting her hand in front of her face and obstructing the light.

'Come out,' said the lady constable as she put a key in the lock.

'Right now?' asked Sameera.

'No. Come out tomorrow!' the lady constable lashed out in anger. 'Of course, I am asking you to come out right now.'

'Okay, I am coming out now,' said Sameera jumping to her feet in case the lady constable changed her mind.

'Your bail has been arranged. You are free to leave for now,' she informed Sameera.

'Bail? How? Who arranged for it?' asked Sameera as she walked out of the holding cell for the first time since coming in.

'Somebody called Alex Matthews.'

29

Love and Other Drugs

Alex Matthews's Diary Entry, 15 August 2025

Dear Diary,

Today is Independence Day! Bowtie Shrink posted a video wearing a tri-coloured bowtie to commemorate the occasion. He suggested that today is the perfect day to seek independence within ourselves from things that are holding us back. The anxieties, the addictions, the trauma . . . Yes! I am going to get freedom too! From living a life below its potential. A sad, love-less life. I had set a plan in motion a few days ago, and it is soon going to play out its conclusion. And I am going to get the sweetest reward for my efforts—Sameera! My darling Sameera! We will be finally together and happy and free.

This is my last diary entry. I am not going to have any time for anything apart from the love of my life. I am going to be completely dedicated to her. Now it is time for the final and most important flashback from my life. It keeps me up at night most often. It scares me and excites me all the same. Without any further ado, lets dive straight into it, starting off from where we last left.

After witnessing the wound Harsh had inflicted on Maya, I spent countless nights and days trying to conjure an idea that would keep her away from him. I had suggested that we elope. We could say goodbye to Harsh, Delhi and this miserable distance between us, and live happily ever after in my native Goa. But the very idea of leaving her urban life behind for a tropical one sent shivers down Maya's spine. She was a city gal. Had always been. Also, there was the additional responsibility of her daughter, Sameera. Maya couldn't abandon her.

Yikes! Sameera was anyway going to be traumatized over her broken family; then why not rip off the bandage completely by letting her stay with her father while Mommy runs away with her Prince Charming? Of course, I never had the guts to express this sentiment in front of Maya. I can only write it in my diary, because who else is ever going to read it except me?

It was a rainy day in July when my prayers were answered. The breakfast buffet had ended an hour ago. The restaurant was empty when Harsh Kapoor walked in and took a seat at the table for two by the window. He demanded pork ribs and a bottle of red wine in his usual entitled manner. It was not a typical order for this time of the day, but then Harsh Kapoor wasn't a typical man either. Some twenty minutes later, I went by his table to make sure everything was all right with his food. The pig had already finished more than three-quarters of the wine and was almost done with the ribs.

I asked if the food was okay and if he needed anything else.

He barked at me to get whiskey for him. Somebody was in the mood to get shit-faced at this time of the day. As I was leaving, he had already put a large chunk of meat in his mouth, and was midway giving me additional instructions: 'Three cubes of . . .'

Except that he couldn't complete the sentence. I asked if he wanted three cubes of ice just out of politeness. But he did not acknowledge this. It was then I realized that something was wrong. His mouth was open, and he was beginning to sweat even though our air conditioners were running at full blast.

Feigning concern, I asked him if he was all right. In my heart, I was jumping with joy.

'Choke . . .' Harsh tried to mouth the word but couldn't bring himself to say it.

I tried to act as normally as possible. I did not want to draw any attention to the situation. 'Sir, what? More wine? More whiskey?' I asked, fully understanding that the man was being choked on his food. I could either beat his back so that his oesophagus could clear off the choked food, or I could rush and call for help. No points for guessing that I chose to do none of the above. There was only one other person in the vicinity at that time, a trainee waiter clearing the table at the other end of the restaurant. He hadn't had the least idea about what was happening. I pretended to laugh and make a false conversation with Harsh Kapoor for the trainee waiter to see. Within a few minutes, I was back in the kitchen, whistling to myself and just going about my work as usual.

An hour later, a sea of people had gathered outside the lobby of The Grand Majestic Hotel. It included policemen, wearing raincoats over their khakis and medical professionals in their green scrubs. Harsh Kapoor, as dead as a dodo, was being stretchered off by a few able-bodied men into a van. It was the most beautiful spectacle of my life. I spotted Maya in the crowd, crying her lungs out. Our eyes met and in that brief second, I smiled at her. Life had found a way for us to be together, at last!

The following few days were a daze for me. I was a happy chimpanzee who had just won a lifetime supply of unlimited bananas. I constantly dreamt about the time Maya, and I would spend together without having to look over our shoulders! How we could now indulge in public displays of affection and how we could now take the next step in our relationship. I dare not say the 'm' word lest I jinx it, but with Harsh Kapoor out of the picture and the universe already on my side, I can dare risk saying it. Marriage! Maya and I would be married and march off into the sunset! But if only reality worked at the same pace as my dreams. I dialled the Presidential Suite late at night, three days after the incident.

'Pumpkin, it is me! How are you doing?' I whispered into the phone.

'I am fine, Alex. How are you?' she asked, her voice exhuasted.

'I am dying to meet you! Shall I come over right now, Pumpkin?' I asked, doing my cute voice.

'No, no, no!' she said immediately. 'Right now, is not good! I'll meet you tomorrow?'

'Okay, okay! No worries! I look forward to meeting you tomorrow, Pumpkin,' I said and kissed her over the phone like we always did at the end of our call.

'Me too,' she said, without returning the kiss.

The obvious and the most logical reason for her behaviour was that she was under tremendous stress after Harsh's death. That man was a dick to her, but he was her husband nevertheless. And they shared a daughter between the both of them. But tomorrow would be a new dawn of our relationship. I couldn't wait for tomorrow.

I was in the restaurant the next day, happily humming to myself while taking a round of the premises before we officially opened for business. I felt a tap on my back. I turned around to see Maya standing in front of me. She was wearing a business pantsuit with medium heels, a novel foray from her usual choice of clothes. Irrespective, she looked like an oasis in the desert. Stunning!

I told her that I didn't hear her come, keeping the tone slightly formal because two of my servers, who were preparing a table, were within earshot. I wanted to hug her and not let her go but these damned servers!

She said she wanted to talk about something in private.

I replied in the affirmative, my heart jumping with joy. Things were about to get saucy. Talk about some midday action! I took her out to the empty balcony which was covered with opaque tarpaulin sheets to keep the rain away.

I hugged her and told her how much I missed her. The fragrance of her signature perfume had a soothing effect on me. It made me forget about the past two days that had passed by without seeing her.

But she freed herself from the hug and looked around to verify that nobody had seen us together. It was all empty. I had made sure of that already. It was understandable to be self-conscious about these things.

I assured her that there was nobody here as I made a second attempt at the hug, which she resisted from the start.

But she firmly told me no, projecting an authoritarian tone, the first time she had ever done that in our relationship. She said that she needed time off to clear her head and that there was a lot happening in her life.

I told her that I understood and attempted to kiss a stray lock of her hair that the breeze had brought close to me. She instantly pulled back. God! Why was she teasing me like this?

She told me that no, I did not understand. Sameera was here from her boarding school, and she didn't want to go back. She wanted to study in Delhi.

But we could still work this out, I assured her for the umpteenth time. The biggest obstacle in our way was out. Everything else was manageable.

She told me that I couldn't even begin to understand the pressure of managing a business like this.

She was angry at the situation that she was in, and she was taking it all out on me. Fair enough. It was the price of being in love.

I repeated a permutation of what I had already told her. It almost sounded like pleading. Did she see my desperation yet?

She told me that she needed some time off, and I knew that there was no point in stretching it further. But the heart wants what it wants. Right? I don't know what came over me. I grabbed her hands back with a ferocity that I had never known existed within me.

'You have no idea about the things that I have done for you,' I told her, anger boiling in my veins.

'Alex, stop,' she cried, trying to free herself. 'You are hurting me! Let go off me!'

But I held on to her hands. Those soft smooth hands that I had dreamt of holding for an entire lifetime . . . I pressed deeper, my nails clawing into her skin. Her eyes swelled and released a single teardrop, which rolled down her cheek and fell on my hand. That is when I released her. She recollected herself for a moment before walking away from that balcony and my life forever. Or so I thought.

Weeks turned into months. Every day I thought that this would be the day when I would receive my marching orders. But the day never came. I saw Maya transform into a successful businesswoman during this time. She dropped her image of a trophy wife and metamorphosed herself into a different persona altogether. I used to bump into her when she hosted business lunches and dinners at my restaurant. We often exchanged formal pleasantries and nothing beyond that. Yet, in our eyes, both of us knew about the unspoken dialogue that had the power to erupt a volcano if expressed.

Months turned into years. My personal life was a mess. I became addicted to anti-depressants. But for what it is worth, my professional life soared to new heights. My restaurant had begun to do exceedingly well and I developed the reputation of a celebrity chef. The hotel was doing much better than the time when Harsh Kapoor was handling it. Even Kapital, the discotheque, was making waves across the city. I had not been with anyone else since Maya. But I knew that she had taken several lovers in the meantime. Nothing serious though, because after seeing them dine at my restaurant for many days in a row, I would suddenly stop seeing these men altogether. Initially, it did sting a lot. But gradually, I made peace with the fact that mine and Maya's love story wasn't a usual one. It was meant to be spread over years and decades and marked by turmoil. As long as I got to see her every other day, I was content. It was a signal that she still wanted me in her life. It was a signal that there was still hope. It was a signal that love always found a way.

Then one day, I got a call on my mobile phone while I was in the kitchen. It was Gyan Singh. He had shifted allegiance to Maya after Harsh.

He skipped the customary hello and got directly to the point. His Boss Madam wanted to see me in the lobby.

Seven minutes later, I found myself seated face to face with my former lover and the forever love of my life, Maya. Maya's bodyguard/personal assistant, Gyan Singh stood at a distance, unable to eavesdrop, still and motionless like a wax statue. An ugly wax statue.

She told me straight up that she was in talks with another chef for a Japanese restaurant in the hotel. Delhi's palate had shifted, and she wanted to capitalize on that trend. She wanted me gone.

These were my marching orders after all. She uttered a few more words, but they were all a blur to me. There may have been an over-explanation about how shutting my ultra-successful and super-famous cash cow of a restaurant in favour of this Japanese gamble was the correct call. So, this is what she had become. An emotionless businesswoman.

I simply said, 'I understand.' Even if I didn't.

She wished me luck for all my future endeavours and gave me a week's time to clear my stuff.

I went home after this little meeting with Maya. As soon as I shut the door behind me, I broke down into a loud tearful cry. I tossed everything around within my sight. The remote control went flying into the television. The flower vase was thrown at the wall, breaking into a hundred tiny pieces. The cushions were torn, and their inner fillings were strewn on the floor. Within ten minutes of my rampage, I had successfully managed to convert my home into a wasteland of destroyed items and dreams. The only thing that kept me moving forward in life was being in the same vicinity as Maya. After she broke off with me, I still had the luxury of loving her from a distance, as I had done for many years since I first saw her. But now she had snatched even that privilege from me. I had given this woman my heart and soul. And in just a five-minute meeting she threw everything down the drain! There had to be consequences for this. I didn't know what, how and when yet, but something had to be done.

The cell phone rang in my pocket. It was a landline call from the hotel. Probably asking to enquire if I had packed my bags yet. But I had till the end of this week. Maybe this was Maya calling to beg for my forgiveness.

I answered the call.

'Chef Alex?' a familiar voice asked.

'Yes,' I replied.

'Chef Alex, this is Sameera Kapoor on this side!' a young chirpy voice said from the other end.

'Ah, yes! Sameera ma'am! How can I help you?' I asked my employer's daughter. Or may I say ex-employer/lover.

'Chef, it is my mother's birthday the day after tomorrow. I am organizing a small surprise party for her tomorrow at midnight at Kapital,' Sameera said.

'That is a great idea,' I said, exuding warmth in my voice.

'Chef, I want you to prepare a chocolate truffle cake for the party. It is her favourite flavour,' she told me.

Of course, I knew what her favourite flavour was, kiddo. I know her like she doesn't even know herself.

'Absolutely! I will prepare the most memorable cake of her life,' I said, grinning ear to ear. *There will be consequences for your actions, Maya Kapoor.*

The next night at the surprise party, Maya saw the ceiling lights fade away. There was complete chaos in the crowd, and in that chaos, I found Sameera crying over her mother's body. She had grown up to be the exact spitting image of Maya when I first met her all those years ago at my Uncle Martin's cafe in Connaught Place. Within this mayhem, I found my north star. God was kind. And love found a way, after all.

30

Worst Proposal of the Century

'Why are we going to Kapital?' asked Sameera as Chef Alex pressed the button to the twentieth floor.

'I need to show you something,' he said.

'How did you manage to bail me out, chef?' asked Sameera as the elevator began its ascend. 'It is the Independence Day weekend, and no magistrate is available.'

'Well, well, well,' said Alex. 'Let us just say that there was a magistrate who liked my nalli nihari so much that he did me a favour.'

Sameera felt nervous from the energy that came from Chef Alex. Why was he behaving so peculiarly? She felt jittery. Maybe she was just exhausted after spending an entire day in jail.

They entered the empty hallway of Kapital through the main entrance.

'Chef, what is it that you want to show me?' asked Sameera, as they crossed the Babylon Bar. 'I have to get on a call with the lawyers. Neil is still out there stuck in jail!'

'I promise you it will be worth the wait,' said Chef Alex as he walked in front of Sameera into the narrow corridor that led to the Grand Stage area. He gestured to her to follow him.

'Chef, what are you doing? We don't have any time to waste! I can't be solving minor issues related to Kapital right now- . . .'

Sameera stopped speaking as soon as she reached the main hall. In the middle of the dance floor was an old chair, and on it, sat a man. A hostage. His hands and legs were thoroughly tied with a rope while a broad roll of duct tape went around his mouth and head. His eyes cried for help.

'Surprise! Surprise!' said Chef Alex, as he presented Bunty Gulati to Sameera akin to a ringmaster presenting a once-wild-but-now-domesticated animal.

'Oh my god! Bunty! You got Bunty in here. He is fit and fine. There are no bandages on him,' exclaimed Sameera in pure euphoria.

'I told you that it will be worth your wait!' said Chef Alex.

'This is amazing!' Sameera was laughing in excitement.

Chef Alex handed his phone to Sameera and said, 'Press play.'

Sameera pressed it and a video began playing. The video featured Bunty.

'My name is Bunty Gulati. I am physically okay. I have no injuries on my body. This is my confession video. I misbehaved with Sameera Kapoor on my birthday which I hosted at Kapital,' said Bunty.

'Explain in detail what you did, you rascal!' growled a voice from behind. It was Alex's.

'I forcibly kissed her and tried to take advantage of her when she was drunk. For this reason, I was beaten up. I completely deserved it. I started a false campaign against her. I portrayed myself as injured and in the hospital, whereas the truth is that I am completely healthy. I even planted the bogus news regarding Sameera Kapoor's insurance scams. Pari Chadha's death was indeed an accident. Sameera Kapoor is innocent.'

The video ended, and there was a big smile on Sameera's face. She hugged Chef Alex.

'Thank you, chef. Thank you!' Sameera was ecstatic. 'What can I ever do to repay you?'

'Marry me!' said Chef Alex, smiling from ear to ear.

'What?' Sameera asked, laughing because she had probably misheard him.

'Marry me!' Chef Alex repeated.

Sameera was no longer laughing.

'Are you out of your mind, chef?' she scoffed. 'It is not the time for such jokes. Come on, we don't have any time to lose. We need to take this confession over the cops right away and get Neil out.'

'Neil! Neil! Neil!' exclaimed Alex, a monstrous rage taking over him. Sameera had never seen the mild-mannered chef speak with such ferocity. 'What do you see in that American fool? Am I not a hundred times better than him?'

Sameera had the urge to throw a truth bomb, but sensing a shift in the power dynamic between her and her employee, she resisted.

'I AM BETTER THAN HIM!' Chef Alex asserted, answering his own question. Why aren't you ready to marry me? What is wrong with me? Haven't I done enough for you?'

Meanwhile, Bunty, struggling to break free from his situation, stopped his efforts after gauging Chef Alex's current mood.

'I . . . I . . . I . . . don't know what to say. I have never looked at you like that,' muttered Sameera.

'You are just like your mother. You neither appreciate me nor my contribution to making your life easier,' said Alex.

'Chef Alex, send me the video, please,' said Sameera, being polite but firm. 'We need to free Neil from the police station. I promise that we will continue this conversation after that.'

'You promise?' asked Alex.

'Yes, I swear,' said Sameera, her breath returning to normal. This was easier than expected.

'I don't give a damn about promises,' said Alex, stomping his foot down on the dance floor. 'Marry me, and you can have the video.'

'Chef Alex, this is no time for your childishness,' Sameera said, showing him who the boss is. 'Give me the video. That is my order!'

'Marry me?' he asked again, making a puppy face this time and almost bending on one knee. 'I know this is the worst proposal of the century, but please give me a chance.'

'No chance in hell!' said Sameera, while a flustered Bunty could not comprehend what was going on.

Alex smiled as he took the phone out from his pocket and pointed the screen towards Sameera.

'There! It is gone forever,' said Alex as he pressed delete on the video. 'No marriage, no video! You can go rot in hell, just like your mother.'

'What is this nonsense, Alex? This is not a bloody joke!' said Sameera. 'I'll take Bunty to the police station and make him confess there.'

'Oh, you will?' asked Alex. 'Let's see how much more he confesses here first.'

Alex removed the tape from Bunty's mouth and whacked him in the head. 'I dare you to confess again, bastard!' he told him.

'You . . . played . . . me,' struggled Bunty with his words and coherence. 'You gave me false information about having Sameera and Neil arrested . . .'

And then the unthinkable happened. Alex removed a gun from his pocket and shot Bunty in the forehead—all within a second. Sameera shrieked so loud that the beer mugs rattled at the Olympus Bar behind them.

'Oh my god! What did you just do?' she said, beginning to wail now that the situation had escalated and how!

'Ah, the art of asking rhetorical questions! You have a lot in common with your mother!' said Chef Alex, as he brushed his shoe against dead Bunty's pants to remove a speck of blood.

There was a faint sound of running footsteps which became louder and more distinct with every passing second. From the narrow corridor appeared Gyan Singh.

'Boss Madam, are you all right?' asked Gyan Singh as he tried to take stock of the scene in front of him. 'I came up to look for you and heard a gunshot!'

Sameera was crying. Bunty sat motionless on a chair with a hole in his head and his brain matter scattered all across the dance floor. And Chef Alex stood with a gun in his hand, looking like a menacing villain.

'Chef Alex killed Bunty!' said Sameera pointing the finger angrily at the perpetrator now that her knight in shining armour had arrived.

'Put that gun down, Alex!' Gyan Singh ordered him.

'Or what?' Chef Alex teased him.

'Or it will be your funeral!' said Gyan Singh, charging towards him.

But Alex was not taking any chances. Not tonight. Not with this lapdog against whom he had harboured decades' worth of grudge. Another gunshot. Another dead body. Gyan Singh was on the floor with a bleeding hole in his throat. Sameera rushed to her fallen soldier.

'No! No! You monster!' cried Sameera, harder than the time when Bunty was shot a few minutes ago. 'You shot Gyan Singh! What has come into you all of a sudden? Why are you doing this?'

Chef Alex came closer to her.

'Come on now, Pumpkin,' he said patting her back, as she tried to find a pulse in Gyan Singh. 'Let us get married without any more melodrama.'

'Don't you dare touch me, asshole!' said Sameera, repulsed. 'You are stupid and naïve enough to think that I'll ever marry you! You disgust me, Alex!'

'There there, Pumpkin,' said Alex unmoved in his resolve to pat her back. 'I am sorry that our beginning was like this. But I promise you that our future will be much better and full of smiles.'

'Wake up, Gyan Singh, wake up,' cried Sameera at the corpse of her bodyguard, paying no heed to Alex. She didn't see him jab a needle into the back of her neck.

31

A Diplomatic Issue

As much as the conditions were unfavourable for a nap, Neil had fallen asleep after all. He woke up with a start when he heard the jail door unlock and swing open. It was hard to see in the limited illumination provided by an only flickering bulb, but Neil was quite sure that the person who was approaching him with restrained footsteps was a suited white man, a Caucasian. He rubbed his eyes to double-check if he was mistaken. He wasn't.

'Mr Ramamurthy? Hi! My name is Eric Woods,' said the white man as he gently placed his briefcase on the bench. He was middle-aged with blond hair and had a hint of a Missouri accent. 'I am from the Embassy of the United States of America in New Delhi. I am handling your case with the Delhi Police.'

These were the sweetest words that Neil had heard ever since Sameera had said 'yes' to his proposal. Mr

Woods was the first American person that Neil had met since coming to India, and he was going to be his saviour!

'And what about Sameera, my fiancé?' said Neil to his only ray of hope in this hellhole. 'She is being held wrongfully as well! You need to get her out too!'

'I am afraid that we do not have any information about your fiancé's situation because she is not a US citizen,' Mr Woods informed him.

'But she will be my wife soon. That will make her a US citizen! You have to help her, Mr . . . sorry I forgot your name,' said Neil.

'I understand your concern, Mr Ramamurthy but at this stage, our hands are tied.'

'Okay,' said Neil, resigning to the reality of the situation. 'Maybe, I will be able to help her once I am out. So, what's the process?'

'We have applied for bail on your behalf to the ambassador. She will review the documents and put her signatures at the bottom. The application will then be submitted to her India counterpart who will also review it and put his signatures. The application will travel to two more departments before we can get you out,' Mr Woods explained.

'So, it is just a couple of signatures! How long shall that take?' enquired Neil, a glimmer of hope in his eyes.

'Not very long ideally . . .' said Mr Woods.

'But? . . .' Neil filled in the gap that Mr Wood had left at the end of the sentence.

'But the US Ambassador is currently in the States for her grandson's baptism. She is back on the day after tomorrow,' revealed Mr Woods.

'And there is absolutely nobody who can sign those damned papers on her behalf?' asked Neil, clasping his sweaty palms together.

'I am afraid not,' came out of the reply.

'But there must be something you can do. Can't you sign the papers? I cannot bear to stay in this place for a single minute,' Neil pleaded.

'Oh no no no!' declared Mr Woods as if Neil had asked for his kidney. 'I cannot sign those papers. That would create a BIG diplomatic issue, and we can't afford one right now.'

'So, I am stuck in this shit hole for two more days!' said Neil, sinking deep into the bench.

'Look, it is just two more days. They will pass like . . .'

'Can you do me a favour, Mr Woods?' asked Neil, interrupting the man who had come to rescue him but not quite.

'Yes?' asked Mr Woods bracing himself for the magnitude of the said favour.

'Can you arrange for me to meet my fiancé, Sameera Kapoor? She is in the women's holding cell in another police station,' said Neil with folded hands. 'Please! I promise that it will be five minutes only!'

'All right, let me see what I can do,' said Mr Woods, realizing that it was something that was within his power to fulfil. 'The officer in charge at the desk seemed like a friendly lad. I don't think he'll mind letting you see your gal for five minutes.'

Neil watched Mr Woods walk out of the holding cell as the guard closed the door behind him. For the first time since being woken up from his nap, Neil looked around the cell. The other bench was empty. His sleeping neighbour whose face he hadn't seen all this while had gone. *Poof!* Like magic. Disappeared into the thin air.

Mr Woods was back as soon as he had left, this time flanked by a young police officer, who Neil assumed was the 'friendly lad.'

'She is no longer there,' said Mr Woods as he entered the holding cell.

'What do you mean "She is no longer there?"' asked Neil.

'Her bail was arranged for, and she left the holding cell about two hours ago,' said the young police officer.

'You must be mistaken. I am talking about Sameera Kapoor. She is an Indian citizen,' said Neil, a million different thoughts taking birth in his brain.

'I am talking about Sameera Kapoor as well. Her bail was arranged for and she left the Saket station premises about two hours ago,' said the officer, patiently repeating the information.

'How's that possible? Who arranged for her bail?' enquired Neil.

'Somebody called Alex Matthews.'

32

Buzzkill

The officers from the day had long gone. The night shift that had taken over the police station had brought an odd sense of calm that KK otherwise did not feel in his line of work. He observed the police station transition from a dragon breathing fire to a stallion quietly jumping through hoops. But to the credit of the day officers, it was not their own choice to be cranky all the time. They constantly had to deal with people who were probably having the worst day of their lives. And well, the general consensus is that nobody ever visits a police station on their good days.

'Boss, tea?' asked the peon as he half-opened the door to KK's cabin holding a stack of small thermocol glasses in one hand and an old plastic thermos in the other.

'No thanks,' said KK.

'It is extra strong. Just the way you like it,' the peon was insistent.

'Fine. Pour me a cup,' said KK.

Once the peon was gone, KK resumed what he was doing before; staring at the evidence that was strewn all across his desk from the Kapital case. There were newspaper clippings titled: `'Fire at Delhi Disco's Opening Night'`, `'Famous Influencer Dies in Freak Accident'`, and a much older faded clipping titled `'Delhi's Stylish Hotelier Dies of Cardiac Arrest at Her Own Club'`. There were photographs of Sameera Kapoor, Maya Kapoor (alive), Maya Kapoor (corpse), Harsh Kapoor (alive), Harsh Kapoor (corpse), Pari Chadha (alive), Pari Chadha (corpse), Bunty Gulati, Neil Ramamurthy, Chef Alex and Gyan Singh. There was something about the case that KK could not wrap his head around. He kept looking at the pictures and newspaper clippings, police reports and autopsy certificates and yet something was missing.

KK's phone buzzed. Maybe it was Bunty trying to reach him with instructions for the remaining five lakh Rupees. That bugger's phone had been unreachable for many hours now. Instead, KK found a WhatsApp message on his phone from a familiar but unsaved contact.

'Having a lonely night, hottie?'

KK clicked on the message, and it opened in his chat window, where he had exchanged a flurry of text messages before with this contact, whose display picture was that of a popular Hindi film actress.

'I am busy right now,' KK wrote back in the chat.

'You can't even spare a little time for me?' came out the reply, which was followed by a wink emoji.

KK shut his phone and kept it on the table. Back to concentrating on the job at hand. There was another text alert from the phone. KK picked it up. The unsaved contact had sent a photograph of a rather busty woman in a tight blouse sitting at the edge of a bed. It was followed by a message:

'Do you want to know what happens next? Pay Rs 299 to find out!'

KK kept the phone down back on the table and returned to the scatter of evidence in front of him. But, less than a minute later, he muttered to himself:

'What the hell!'

He picked up the phone and sent Rs 299 to the contact via Paytm. As soon as he had done that, he received a video file on WhatsApp. He pressed play, but his phone displayed a 'Storage full, please delete old files to create space' message. How frustrating! KK opened his media gallery and selected a bunch of random photographs to delete. In the middle of these photographs, there was a video file whose thumbnail he didn't recognize. He pressed play. The video from the night when he was caught prying around on the hidden floor in Kapital began playing. Between his angry boss and the stress of suspension, he had completely forgotten about it. He watched intently as a potential clue revealed itself.

Sameera woke up in a blur. She wanted to rub her eyes only to realize that her hands and legs were tied to a chair. Where was she? Everything felt so familiar and yet so different. It looked like the Grand Stage area of Kapital at first glance, but the set-up seemed a bit different. She wanted to shout and yell for help, but her throat couldn't do better than producing a hoarse whisper.

'There, there, Pumpkin! Don't exert yourself. You have got to stay fresh for your big day! *Our* big day to be precise,' said Alex as he appeared in front of her, holding a bright maroon shade of lipstick in his hand.

Sameera realized that he looked different as well. He was wearing a black tuxedo over a white frill shirt with a red-velvet bow tie. His hair was parted perfectly into a side crease. His perfume was overpowering, reminding her of the jail disinfectant that made her instantly nauseous. It was a crime against her sense of smell. She had mostly seen Alex in his chef's uniform and sometimes in normal civilian clothes. To even think that he owned a tux was preposterous.

'Please let me go,' Sameera said, her voice barely audible.

'Let you go? That would defeat the entire purpose of everything I ever did!' said Chef Alex as he paced himself forward and backward in front of her. Sameera noticed a slight tremble in his hands.

'Please let me go, I beg you, Alex!' said Sameera, as her voice gained a slight more intensity.

'Sweetheart! Sweetheart! Sweetheart!' said Alex, as he ran his hand in her hair. 'Come on, don't be a buzzkill! By the way, I learnt that word from your mother!'

Sameera felt her heart stop. 'My mother?' The situation was becoming more bizarre with every successive dialogue exchange.

'Yes, Pumpkin! Your mother, Maya. My Maya! My beautiful Maya, the love of my life,' said Alex with a wicked grin.

And before Sameera could ask him to elaborate further, Alex did the honours himself.

'I fell in love with your mother the very first time I saw her, at my Uncle Martin's café,' he said, talking slowly and articulately. 'But she was already married to that human turd, Harsh Kapoor. I discovered that they owned a hotel and were passionate about food. So, I trained myself as a professional chef and somehow joined the culinary team at The Grand Majestic Hotel. I was happy loving your mother from afar. Something is better than nothing, right? Over the years, your father showed his true colours. He started having affairs and beating your mother up regularly.'

'You are a liar! My father would do nothing of that sort,' said Sameera, anger giving her vocal cords a new lease of life.

'Oh, but he did, Pumpkin! He beat the lights out of your mother,' said Alex dreamily. 'Harsh Kapoor, however charming and classy he appeared in front of the world, the truth is that he was a stone-cold wifebeater! I rescued your mother when she had taken a rather vicious beating from him. And thus began our beautiful relationship!'

'You are a bloody liar! I don't believe you!' shouted Sameera at him, trying in vain to break free from the ropes. 'My mother would never be with somebody like *you*!'

'Oh, but she was, Pumpkin! She was! Do you know that once your mother and I made love in this very club? Over there, behind the Olympus Bar, when everybody had left. Oh! What a sweet, sweet time it was,' said Alex, closing his eyes to recreate the treasured moment.

'You are disgusting!' said Sameera, spitting a mouthful of saliva in his direction.

'You will not understand, Pumpkin. You have not experienced true love in your life.'

'True love?' asked Sameera, bewildered and disgusted. 'What would you know anything about true love? Nobody could ever love a pathetic person such as yourself!'

'I used to think that about myself too, Pumpkin, until Maya drowned me in the ocean of her love . . .'

'Bullshit!' yelled Sameera at the top of her lungs. 'You are lying! What proof do you have?'

'Proof? You want proof?' asked Alex, excited to reveal the next bit of information. 'If you want proof, then why don't you ask your father? Oh wait, I completely forgot that he is long dead. And do you know how and why? It was me! I did it for love. I did it for Maya, my love. What bigger proof do you need?'

'You killed my father?' asked Sameera but it was more a statement than a question, as a fresh stream of tears geared up for discharge at any moment now.

'Let us just say that I had the opportunity to save him, and I did not. It was an act of God. But your mother, instead of thanking me, became aloof and distant,' said Chef Alex, sounding heartbroken. 'But, I was given a new chance at love . . . With you! I am so mesmerized that I want nothing else from the universe apart from you! And I have finally made that happen by removing all obstacles in our way, Pumpkin.'

'What obstacles?' asked Sameera.

'Come on, Pumpkin. I think you are smarter than that. Take a wild guess?' said Alex smirking. 'Hint, it happened right over here in Kapital.'

'You were responsible for all of those strange events?' asked Sameera in disbelief.

'Strange events for you,' said Alex. 'They were a necessity to restore order in the universe for me. I started the fire on the opening night because I could not bear you getting close to Neil. And on the night of Neil's proposal, what happened to that girl was my doing . . .'

'Pari? Why did she have to die? Did she reject you as well? No wonder!'

'Pari Chadha was, well, she was just unlucky. Collateral damage. Wrong place, wrong time,' said Alex, without any guilt or remorse. 'I saw your boyfriend proposing to you on the stage. My first instinct was to unscrew a disco light directly above the stage where he was. But I realized that it could have harmed you as well. And I could not risk losing two loves of my life in the same lifetime. I couldn't, right?'

Alex paused for effect.

'So, in a fit of rage, I unscrewed a random stage light above the crowd, and poor Pari was the chosen one. Alas! The real tragedy was that by the time the light fell, you had already said "yes", and that American moron had already put the ring on your finger,' said Alex.

'You could have come directly to me,' she screamed at him. 'You did not need to do what you did!'

'And what would you have done?' he asked, bending down to be face-to-face with her. 'Embraced me? Or fired me from the hotel and your life forever?'

'But violence wasn't the answer, Alex . . .'

'I did try to scare your American boyfriend away by jamming his elevator, so you cannot say that I did not try to prevent this carnage,' said Alex, breaking into laughter.

Sameera was speechless after what she had heard. She wanted to wail and cry but did not want to project herself as weak in front of this monster. Alex's phone rang. He answered it and then kept it back within a second.

'It is time, Pumpkin,' he told her.

'Time for what?' she asked.

'Time for us to be united in the eyes of God,' he said, coming closer and opening the stick of lipstick that he had been holding in his hand for a while.

'A little touch-up and you will be good to go,' he said as he forcefully smudged the lipstick on her lips. It came on unevenly as if someone had used a wide brush to paint over the fence.

Alex turned Sameera around 180 degrees in her chair to face the DJ stage. This is when Sameera realized why Kapital had a different vibe to it when she first regained consciousness. Strings of fairy lights were hanging all around the walls and ceiling. The dance floor was littered with red heart-shaped balloons. On the DJ stage above, an iPad was made to stand like a photo frame, and its screen showed a bald white man in priestly robes, looking directly at Sameera and Alex.

'Pumpkin, this is Father Carlos. He is from Costa Rica. I found him online. Father Carlos is going to get us married tonight. Say hello to him!'

Horror dawned upon Sameera. She looked down at herself, at some point while being unconscious, she had been changed into a white Catholic wedding dress.

'Sir, I request you. Please help me,' cried a frantic Neil, holding the bars and trying to shake them dramatically.

'How many times do I have to tell you? I cannot give you my mobile again,' said the annoyed night guard, who was trying to peacefully watch the cricket match on his cellphone. 'You have already used it twice. Both times your girlfriend's number came as switched off.'

'Sir, please, one last time,' said Neil, letting go of the bars and folding his hands together, which in his short stay so far in India, he had discovered to be a very useful hand gesture. 'It is very unlike her to switch the phone off and not contact me while I am stuck here. Something is wrong!'

'Listen, you could get me in trouble if I gave you my phone again. It is against the rules,' said the guard softening up a little bit. The folded hand gesture worked. He looked around to make sure that nobody was watching and snuck his phone to Neil through the bars.

'Two minutes only,' the guard warned him. Neil said a quick thank you and went behind the small wall partition inside the holding cell, which had an Indian-style commode and a tiny wash basin. He dialled Sameera's phone number and waited for her to pick up.

'The number you are trying to reach is either switched off or not reachable,' informed the phone service.

'Fuck! Fuck! Fuck!'

Neil examined the digits. They were correct. He had learnt Sameera's phone number by heart a long time ago. So, Sameera's phone was switched off. What else could he do? Who else could he call? He did not know anybody's number except for his mom's but there was no point in calling her in Boston and informing her that he was stuck in an Indian jail while his fiancé was MIA. Neil had a lightbulb moment. There was a slight possibility that it would work. He opened the browser, searched for The Grand Majestic Hotel on Google, and clicked on the phone number listed below. The call connected almost instantaneously. But to a pre-recorded machine bot.

'Good evening, you have reached the official line of The Grand Majestic Hotel. Press 1 for Hindi and 2 for English.'

Gosh! He wanted to speak to a real human being and not a pre-recorded computer message. He pressed 2 anyway. That choice was a no-brainer.

'For fresh bookings, press 1. To view or edit your confirmed bookings, press 2. To speak to our concierge, press 3. To book a . . .'

Neil pressed 3. Another no-brainer.

'Please stay on the line as we connect your call to the hotel.'

Neil waited while a jazz tune played on the call. In any other circumstance, he would have appreciated the music.

'Thank you for calling The Grand Majestic Hotel. This is Divya. How may I help you?'

'Divya! This is Neil on this side! Your boss Sameera's fiancé.'

There was a momentary silence at the other end before Divya spoke again.

'Sir, this is The Grand Majestic Hotel in New Delhi. Are you sure you have the right number?'

'Divya, it is me, Neil, Sameera's fiancé!' said Neil hurriedly. 'Don't you remember that I was with Sameera last month when she came to the reception and asked you to make a fresh key card for the Presidential Suite?'

'Neil, sir? Is that you?' said Divya after another momentary pause that seemed like forever.

'Yes, Divya it is me! I need you to do something for me. Find Sameera and . . .'

Before Neil could finish his sentence, the phone was snatched away from his hand.

'Your two minutes are up!' said the guard as he disconnected the call and put the phone back in his pocket.

33

Lost in Translation

The sole attendees to the wedding of the century, besides the reluctant bride, the eager groom and the foreign priest, were the dead bodies of Gyan Singh and Bunty Gulati. Alex, the ecstatic groom, was kneeling on the floor of the DJ stage with his bride's hands locked in his own. His bride, Sameera, was still tied to her chair. She felt nauseous from the taste of the godawful lipstick that Alex had plastered on her lips, a vile vomit imminent. Father Carlos, the priest from Costa Rica who was present at the ceremony through the wonders of technology was reciting some lines from the Bible, albeit in Spanish.

'*Compromiso para unirse en matrimonio*,' said the Father, reading from a thick cardboard-bound red book [Commitment to join in marriage].'

'Father Carlos! This wedding is happening against my will. You have to inform the authorities in India to come to the Kapital Club at The Grand Majestic Hotel in New Delhi! NOW!' cried Sameera out loud in a single breath.

In acknowledgement, Father Carlos smiled at her through the iPad and continued to speak.

'*Tal como dice esa canción estamos aquí para celebrar un amor como ese. Ese amor en el que uno no puede imaginarse la vida sin el otro.* [Just like the song says, we are here to celebrate an eternal love. The love in which one cannot imagine life without the other].'

'Don't waste your energy, Pumpkin,' said Alex, gently stroking her hair. 'Father Carlos only understands Spanish,'.

'Father Carlos! I need help,' said Sameera in open rebellion to her groom's advice.

Father Carlos was unaffected by her cries for help. Sameera's decision to choose Mandarin over Spanish as an additional subject in school was here to haunt her now for the rest of her life.

'Don't worry, Pumpkin, it will be over soon,' said Alex.

'*El amor que se tienen uno al otro se siente como un principio y a la vez un final.* [The love you have for each other feels like a beginning and at the same time an end].'

'You asshole, what do you think?' Sameera lashed out at Alex. 'You will marry me forcefully through some bogus online priest, and we will live happily ever after?'

'But Pumpkin . . .' Alex tried to pacify Sameera.

'You are forgetting that you are in Kapital in The Grand Majestic Hotel. How do you think you will escape from here? You will have to cross the lobby and the security along with me,' said Sameera, changing her demeanour from a damsel in distress to the boardroom bully she loved to be. She could see that Alex was rattled. She would have to continue with this strategy. 'The cleaning crew is scheduled to arrive here in a few hours. So, the option of staying here forever is also out.'

'Hush, Pumpkin! We can talk later,' said an unperturbed Alex. 'Don't let Father Carlos off this rhythm.'

'*Estamos aquí para apoyar y honrar este gran amor entre Alex y Sameera.* [We are here to support and honor this great love between Alex and Sameera].'

'My mother never loved you. She just used you to get rid of my father,' said Sameera, a defiant fire blazing in her eyes. This time the smile vanished from Alex's face.

'What did you say, Pumpkin?' asked Alex.

'My mother just used you to get rid of my father,' repeated Sameera. 'And you thought it was love? Men can be such fools!'

'It was love! Real love!' said Alex. 'I know it in my heart.'

'Was it? Then why did she distance herself from you after my father's death?' asked Sameera who knew that even though she was the one tied up, the reins of this conversation had fallen in her hands.

'She distanced herself because . . . because she wanted to focus on you! You were a kid at that time. Moreover, she wanted to . . . focus on this hotel business of hers,' said Alex, struggling to find words in between.

Sameera broke into furious laughter, 'You are so naïve, Alex Matthews!'

'That is the truth!' pleaded Alex, like a small kid trying to convince his mother that there indeed was a monster in his closet.

'The truth is that after my father's death, you were of no use to her,' said Sameera, rejoicing in her new strong avatar. 'She let you stay and run the restaurant because it had become popular. I'll have to give it to my mother, what a fantastic businesswoman she was!'

Alex was sweating profusely now. The gigantic Grand Stage Hall suddenly felt hot and suffocating to him. Father Carlos was reciting his verses from Costa Rica in the background, unfazed by the escalating conversation in Delhi.

'Los dos han llegado aquí a comprometerse de ahora en adelante [The two of you have come here to commit to each other from now on].'

'Stop it!' cried Alex. 'I said stop!'

He stood up to his feet, picked up the iPad and tossed it far away in the club. Father Carlos fell silent.

'You are lying!' said Alex to Sameera. 'You are saying all of this to get in my head!'

'Am I?' Sameera asked. Alex's outburst scared her but she dared not show it right now.

'Shut up! Just shut up! Not a word more!' said Alex, who was now walking to and fro along the length of the DJ stage in visible frustration.

'You were a loser then. You are a loser now. Poor little loser,' said Sameera, her voice taking on a childish voice intended to mock him.

Smack! Smack! Smack!

'Shut up, bitch!' said Alex after delivering three tight slaps on her face.

Sameera felt the blood release slowly from the inside of her cheeks and trickle into the rest of her mouth. Her tastebuds were now overwhelmed by a cocktail of cheap lipstick mixed with her own blood, courtesy of Chef Alex.

'You can marry me all you want by forcefully tying me up. But that is all you can ever do in life,' said Sameera as she spat some of the blood from her mouth on the dance floor. 'You will never find a real woman who will love you and be ready to be your wife of her own accord.'

Alex stomped his feet on the ground.

'This is enough! Not a word out of your mouth, bitch.' he said, taking out the gun from his pocket. 'You are just like your mother. Heartless and cruel.'

'Oh yeah? Just because she and I did not fancy a pathetic loser like yourself? Then so be it!' said Sameera, feeling braver than ever despite seeing the gun in Alex's hand.

Thump! Alex hit her on the head with the grip of the gun. It hurt like she had smashed her skull against a concrete wall. The pain was only mild at first but within seconds it became unbearably excruciating. She could feel her mind fading away, but she knew that she would have to break him further.

'You are a loser!' she slurred as she fought with her fleeting consciousness. 'A big stupid loser!'

'This is it, bitch. I am going to watch you die just like I watched your mother die right over here in this club,' said Alex, his gun pointed at Sameera.

There was a deafening sound. Alex fell knees first on the ground, his white shirt turned red under the tuxedo, a colour matching his bowtie. The last thing Sameera saw in the haze of unconsciousness was Neil rushing to her, and Inspector KK standing over Alex with a gun.

34

Happily Ever After

Six Weeks Later

The morning rush at the District Court Complex was as busy as Inspector KK had expected, as he made his way through the crowd. Exactly ten 'excuse mes' and five 'sorrys' later, he finally reached Courtroom 12 on the second floor. Unlike the other courtrooms that KK had passed on his way, Courtroom 12 was the only one that could boast of harbouring happy citizens. Some of them were even giggling and posing for photographs as they came out in pairs. KK recalled the time when many years ago he too had come to this anomaly of a courtroom as a starry-eyed young man fresh out of college.

'Inspector KK, we weren't expecting you!' said Neil as he bumped into the policeman at the entrance.

'I came to extend my congratulations! Where is Ms Kapoor?' asked KK.

'Well, she is Mrs Ramamurthy now,' said Neil, showing off the garland around his neck. 'Sam is over there, talking to my mother.'

KK saw Sameera, with a similar garland around her neck engaged in an animated conversation with a tall grey-haired lady in the corner.

'Oh, okay. I'll just go say congratulations and be on my way back,' said KK.

'Sure. Come with me,' said Neil as he and KK walked over to the ladies.

A wide smile appeared on Sameera's face when she saw her husband walking towards her along with her once-foe-now-saviour.

'How nice of you to come visit us, Inspector KK!' she said.

KK observed her face. Most of the bruises were gone since he'd last met her a few weeks ago. The wounds on her scalp had seemed to have healed as well.

'Congratulations, Ms Kapoor or uhm Mrs Ramamurthy as your husband has instructed me to call you,' said KK, with a half-laugh at his own joke.

'Thank you, inspector. You are the reason that I am alive today,' said Sameera with utmost sincerity.

'You should really thank your husband. He raised a ruckus in jail, sensing something was wrong much before I had any idea,' said KK, pointing to Neil who was standing beside him, going red in the praise.

'You can say that I have a superb taste in men!' said Sameera, which made Neil blush even more.

'My son finally did something worthwhile—save this lovely girl so that she could become my daughter-in-law,' said Neil's mother who had been quiet ever since the policeman walked in and interrupted the precious one-on-one conversation with her brand-new daughter-in-law.

'Come on, Maa!' said Neil, a tad embarrassed.

'Your mother is right,' said Sameera joining in the playful bashing of her husband along with her mother-in-law. 'And the best thing that you did for me, Neil, was to give me a second chance of having a wonderful mother again. Do you know, Inspector KK, that Mom immediately flew to India from Boston when she heard about my incident? She has been taking care of me ever since.' Sameera's eyes had swelled up a little.

Neil's mother got up from her chair and kissed Sameera on her forehead. 'I am always there for you. Don't you ever forget that,' she said.

'I will not, Mom,' said Sameera and the two of them held each other's hands.

'I guess I should be on my way now,' said KK, not wanting to make this warm family moment awkward by his presence.

Nobody said anything and that was dialogue enough that yes, they agreed that he should be on his way. As KK was nearing the exit of Courtroom 12, Neil came rushing behind him, and called out, 'Inspector KK! Please stop for a second.'

'Yes, Mr Ramamurthy.'

'I had a question that I have not been able to wrap my head around ever since the incident,' said Neil.

'Shoot! I'd be happy to answer any query that you have,' replied the policeman.

'How did you know that it was Chef Alex?'

KK paused for a second before answering. 'Honestly, I had a very strong hunch that something about this case did not make sense. I had made a video when I was caught snooping around at Kapital,' said KK, and Neil crossed his arms in guilt as he recalled how the snooping incident had been dealt with.

'Anyway,' continued the Inspector. 'I had completely forgotten about that video until much later when I came across it in my media gallery. I played it on a whim. In the video, I came across a dirty white handkerchief thrown in the corner of the false floor above the club. First, I thought nothing of it. Then I zoomed in on it. The pixels were quite grainy, you know, with this old phone of mine,' KK said holding his phone up for Neil to see.

'And then?' asked Neil.

'I then realized that it was too big for a normal handkerchief. It was circular, which was unusual too. I was chasing this train of thought when my subordinate came to my office bearing two pieces of news: *one*, that Sameera's bail had been arranged by Chef Alex Matthews and *two*, that you were creating a ruckus in your holding cell about wanting to speak to her,' said KK.

'Ha ha! Thank god for the ruckus,' said Neil.

'It just struck me that the circular handkerchief in the video was a chef's hat. Chef Alex's hat. It was just one coincidence too many,' said KK, as he walked out of Courtroom 12, leaving the newlywed groom at the entrance.

'I don't want anything fancy. And please keep me away from The Grand Majestic Hotel today,' Sameera had given clear instructions when Neil had asked, 'How do you want to celebrate today?'

Therefore, the after-party was a small affair, which considering the scale of the wedding earlier in the day, wasn't unexpected. Neil had chosen Show Lé, a small pub in Hauz Khas Village as the venue. Hauz Khas Village or HKV as woke Delhites liked to call it, was a quaint little South Delhi neighbourhood with two distinct halves. The first half boasted of alleys littered with designer boutiques selling their esoteric merchandise during the day, and bars and restaurants blasting their loud music during the night. The other half consisted of a park, a morning destination for joggers and laughter yoga club members alike, and a small lake in its centre.

Show Lé buzzed with laughter, music and good vibes. A childhood friend of Sameera had just finished recounting a very embarrassing story from the time when Sameera had tried to sneak out from her boarding school at night to meet a boyfriend, her plan foiled only when she had been caught red-handed by the dean. The story was received with a lot of hooting and playful jibing as Sameera tried to bury her face in her hands.

Neil's mother began to narrate an embarrassing anecdote from his childhood, but he was able to successfully nip that attempt in the bud. Somebody informed the pub DJ that a freshly married couple were in the house. The DJ responded by playing *All Out of Love* by Air Supply and inviting the couple on the floor for a slow dance. The crowd from the wedding after-party cheered as Neil held Sameera gently by the waist and began their official first dance.

By the time Sameera came back to the table, there were four missed calls on her phone. All from Emily. Sameera picked up the fifth call as it rang in her hands.

'You missed my wedding, bitch!' said Sameera before Emily even had the chance to say 'hello'.

'I know, I am sorry babe,' replied her best friend from across the globe. 'But to be fair, you didn't give me enough time, and my dream of being an Indian bridesmaid is ruined forever.'

'I *did* tell you!' Sameera pestered.

'Yeah, you did, but only like three days ago,' retorted Emily. 'For some of us, it would take a twenty-hour flight to reach Delhi. You see?'

'Mea culpa! I am sorry,' said Sameera, accepting her mistake. 'It just happened so fast! Neil's Mom has been here for a while. She is so supportive and loving that words are not enough. She encouraged us to get married soon and put the events of the recent past behind us. And I think that it was the right call.'

'It was the right call indeed, girl!' pressed Emily. 'And I am so happy for you!'

'Thank you, Em,' said Sameera. 'I miss you.'

'I miss you too, Sam,' said Emily, taking a slight pause. 'There is something that I wanted to talk to you about, but it seems to me you are in the middle of your wedding party right now. Let me call you over the weekend.'

'No, no, tell me now!' said an intrigued Sameera, as she stepped into an alley through the pub's backdoor, which overlooked the lake. 'It is much quieter here, and I could use a break from the constant smiling. Gosh, my cheeks hurt so bad!'

'Perils of being a newlywed bride,' babbled Emily.

'I see your sense of humour is taking a dip. Now, come on! Fill me in with the goss!' demanded Sameera, as she walked past a closed gluten-free bakery.

'Okay, so I was in New York recently, for a business conference,' said Emily, without being prompted again.

'Yes, you told me! Where you hooked up with a cute guy who turned out to be married!' snorted Sameera.

'Yes, that happened,' admitted Emily. 'But . . .'

'Don't tell me you are seeing him again, Em!' said Sameera. 'This has a big red flag written all over it!'

'No, it is not about him,' said Emily. 'There's something else.'

'Hmm?'

'I was at the JFK International Airport in New York after the conference, waiting to board my flight back to Vancouver,' said Emily, her breathing becoming a little heavier. 'When I saw a news flash on the TV. The police had managed to identify a previously unknown dead body that they had discovered in the sewers a few months ago.'

Sameera was silent. She waited for her friend to elaborate to be able to make sense of this information. Emily continued with her story.

'I thought I recognized the name of the victim from somewhere but couldn't place it. Anyway, I boarded my flight and didn't think much of it. But last night, I had a sudden brainwave. I remembered where I recognized the name from. I opened our chats from November last year, and my hunch was right.'

'Don't keep me in suspense, girl,' said Sameera. 'Spill the beans!'

'The victim was Rohan Khanna,' said Emily, jumping to the point and ripping off the bandage.

'Rohan, who?' asked Sameera, but she remembered as soon as the words came from her mouth.

'You know who,' said Emily. 'Your Hinge date.'

'But how's that possible?' asked Sameera, not sure if she had heard her friend a gazillion miles across the world correctly on the phone.

'It is true, Sam,' said Emily somberly. 'Rohan Khanna is dead. I verified his photograph from the news and the screenshot that you sent me.'

'What? How is that even possible? When did this happen?' asked a confounded Sameera as she stopped in the middle of an alley.

'He was apparently mugged, killed and dumped in Brooklyn by two masked assailants, who were never caught,' informed Emily.

'And when did this happen?' asked Sameera.

'Umm, let me check. The news article is open on my computer. It happened in the afternoon of 5 November.'

'5 November?'

'Yes, 5 November.'

'No, this cannot be true! I was waiting for him at a club in Brooklyn on 5 November! How did I not know about this?' Sameera asked her friend while trying to process the news. 'Oh my god! He didn't ghost me. He was in trouble and he would have expected me to look for him . . .'

'Rohan had no ID on him when his body was discovered. His face was beaten to a pulp and beyond recognizable. The police had no way of contacting his friends and family. Everybody just assumed Rohan had gone off the grid to trek in a forest like he had done many times before,' said Emily, reading from the news article without any emotions.

'Oh my god, Em! And all this while I thought that he had chickened out of the date,' said Sameera, her hands trembling.

'I shouldn't have given you this news today,' said Emily, visibly disturbed herself. 'I am sorry for ruining your wedding day. Oh my god, I feel so guilty,'

'No, it is okay, Em. Thank you for telling me. Listen, Neil is calling me back inside. I'll talk to you tomorrow?' Sameera lied to her best friend.

'Are you sure, Sam?' enquired Emily. 'God! I feel so guilty!'

'Yes, Em,' said Sameera. 'Don't worry about it. I really have to go. Neil is calling for me.'

'Okay, please enjoy your night,' said Emily, still doubting the timing of her news. 'Give my love to Neil!'

'I will!' said Sameera as she began walking in the narrow alleyway, not sure where she was headed.

There was no way she was going back inside without processing what she had just learnt. A barrage of million different thoughts ran through her head. Rohan Khanna was dead all this while, and she had no idea about it. She knew that he was a nature nerd, and their first meeting was actually fun, and she looked forward to the second date throughout the week. If she had cared to enquire about him, maybe his body would have been identified sooner. If she had not chosen the club in Brooklyn, he would still have been alive.

'Sam, babe! Where are you going?' called out the most comforting voice in the universe. 'Come on, everybody is waiting for you inside!' It was Neil, breaking her reverie.

Sameera stopped walking only to realize that she had reached the other half of Hauz Khas through the alleys. It was the park that was extensively spread across hundreds of acres. From here, the music from the pubs was only a faint echo. The chirping of the crickets and the gentle waves in the lake under the full moon were the only dominating sounds now. In different circumstances, she would have appreciated this rare spectacle of serenity in Delhi. Sameera rushed to Neil and began crying in his chest as he held her close.

'What happened, babe?' asked Neil. "Is everything all right? Who were you talking to on the phone?'

'It was Emily,' said Sameera, making his shirt damp with her tears. 'She just told me about the death of an old friend of mine.'

'Oh god! I am so sorry, Sam. Are you all right?' he asked, gently rubbing her head.

'I don't know, Neil. I really don't,' said Sameera, struggling to find the right words. 'I've been trying to put everything that has happened recently behind me. But I don't think I am strong enough to handle another devastating news.'

'Is there anything that I can do to make you feel better?' asked Neil but received no response from his sobbing wife.

'Was this a close friend?' Neil followed up when he received no coherent reply to the previous question.

'He was . . . he wasn't,' said Sameera, still at a loss for words. 'I don't know.'

'It is okay, babe. I'm here for you,' he said, stroking her hair as she clung to him. 'Don't exert yourself. Talk whenever you are ready. Remember, your therapist has advised you to express your emotions as they come!'

'I had met him, the friend who died, online on Hinge,' Sameera finally said, looking up at her husband.

'Sorry, what?' Neil was astonished and rightly so. 'Were you guys a couple?'

'No, we went on just a single date,' told Sameera. 'On the second date I was waiting for him, but he never showed up. I thought he had stood me up, but it turns out he got mugged and killed on his way to meet me. It was the same day I met you in New York City.'

A fresh stream of tears rolled down her cheeks.

'I am such a terrible person for not following up after him. If I did, he probably would have survived. It is all my fault that he's dead,' she said.

'Babe, you could never have known that. You cannot blame yourself. It is unfair,' said Neil, looking directly into her eyes.

'Neil, I think you should leave me,' said Sameera breaking free from the cocoon of his arms.

'Sam, darling, what are you saying?' asked Neil, bowled over by that request on their wedding day.

'I am cursed, Neil,' she said, taking a step back from him. 'Can't you see? Everybody who comes into my life ends up getting hurt or killed. I can't do that to you or your mom, Neil. I can't . . .'

'Babe, your one-date-boyfriend getting mugged and dying outside a club, is a pure twist of fate. That's it,' said Neil trying to put some sense into her.

Sameera chewed the nail off her pinkie finger as a cloud of awkward momentary silence danced between them.

'Plus, you got to look at the brighter side,' said Neil. 'Him getting mugged wasn't entirely bad. It is a dark thing to say, but if he had made it to your date that day, we wouldn't be together today. Do you remember that you were sitting by yourself at the table and waiting for him while I was the designated DJ? I dedicated a song to you . . . 'the cute girl who shouldn't be sitting by herself.' And the rest as we say is history!' Neil was smiling from ear to ear.

'And you played "Drive By" by Train, my favourite song in the entire world!' exclaimed Sameera, her mood lighter now.

'The stars have never aligned so perfectly!' said Neil.

Sameera relaxed her shoulders and let out a deep exhale. 'Maybe I'm thinking too much into it. I am sorry, Neil, I am such a mess on our wedding day. You deserve better,' she said, holding his hand into hers.

'Hey! Hey! Babe!' He said, putting his finger on her lips. 'You are a beautiful mess, and it is my privilege to spend the rest of my life together with you.'

They kissed as the full moon cast its complete reflection onto the Hauz Khas lake behind them. The faint echo of music from the pubs was completely drowned by the sound of crickets chirping. Neil picked Sameera's slender frame up from the ground as passion engulfed both the lovers.

'Neil! Neil!' said Sameera, trying to break away from the embrace. But her husband seemed to be in little mood for talking.

'Neil!' she nudged him hard, enough to get him to reply.

'What babe?' he asked.

'How did you know "Drive By" by Train was my favourite song?' she asked.

'What?'

'At the club, when my date stood me up, how did you know that "Drive By" was my favourite song? We had never met until then,' she enquired.

'Babe, it was such a long time ago. I honestly don't remember,' he said, trying to resume the interrupted kiss, but Sameera wasn't done just yet.

'Try to remember, please? For me?' she asked again.

'Babe, I think it was just one happy coincidence,' he said, trying not to sound frustrated. 'I was going to play that song anyway and I took my chance with the cute girl sitting by herself. Satisfied?'

'But how on earth can this be a coincidence?' she asked, breaking free from him and moving backwards. 'My date ghosts me, and while I am waiting for him, an Indian DJ plays my favourite song dedicated to me! Inspector KK says, "One coincidence is too many."'

'Babe, where is this coming from? That bumbling fool of an inspector has made you paranoid. Why are you behaving like this? Come on, it is our wedding day!' he said, reaching the upper limits of his patience.

Sameera breathed out a big sigh of ease as she came closer to her husband and said, 'I am sorry, Neil. I don't know what has gotten into me. I can't think clearly at all. Please take me away from here. Somewhere far away from this city.'

'I will, Sam,' said Neil, locking in his arms. 'And you know what, babe? If you had dated that loser who got mugged and killed, it wouldn't have worked out anyway with him or anybody else because you are a fucking task to handle with all your mood swings and melodrama!'

'Neil, what are you . . .' Sameera asked as she tried to make sense of the sudden shift in her husband's tone, but her words were annihilated as Neil smothered her in his hug.

'Sameera, you are a fucking piece of work. But thank goodness that this is the last time I had to tolerate your nonsense!' said Neil, his grip around Sameera getting tighter.

'Neil, stop! Neil, stop,' she tried to protest but all in vain. He was too strong to overpower. But she realized that she had one tried and tested method to get out of this situation. She kicked him in the balls, and Neil shrieked in agony and let go of her.

'Neil, tell me this is not true! Tell me that this is some sick joke of yours!' Sameera said.

'Oh, but this is all true, darling!' said Neil, recovering from the kick and settling into his role as the newly revealed devilish villain of the story.

'But why?' asked Sameera, her eyes red with trauma and betrayal.

'The "why", my darling, is the least interesting part of this all. You should really focus on the "how" and the "when!"'

'The "how" and the "when?" Neil, what are you saying? I cannot understand anything . . .'

'You will understand everything, Sam. I have been itching to tell you this for so long,' said Neil, a monstrous confidence on his face while Sameera shivered on her spot. 'We had been planning this for decades."

'Who is "we?" And decades? But we have only known each other for a few months . . .'

'I have known you since forever, sweetheart,' said Neil. 'I have kept a diligent track of your likes and dislikes, your taste in music and films, political leanings, and whatnot; everything to *groom* myself into becoming a man worthy of you. Hell, I even became a DJ because I knew that it would come in handy at Kapital. I wasn't wrong, wasn't I?'

'Neil, who are you? Why are you doing this? Tell me that all of this is nothing but a joke!'

'It is all a part of a carefully crafted plan,' said Neil. 'And it was all going smoothly until that stupid Chef Alex came into the picture. I could have become a rich man much sooner and avoided the unnecessary bloodshed. But, alas, sweet wife, I have told you enough now, and I can't let you live.'

'You did all of this for my wealth? For my money?' Sameera asked. 'I thought you were better than that, Neil. I would have given you money if you had simply asked me!'

'Look at you, poor little rich girl throwing words as if it were wads of cash because they are all the same to you!' he said, mocking her act of defiance.

'Answer me, Neil! Did you ever love me?' she demanded of her husband but instead of receiving an answer, she received a slap. And another one. And another one. And another one. Left. Right. Center. Till the time she was barely conscious. The stitches had opened up. A slow trickle of blood began pouring out of her head. Her vision was spinning at a supersonic speed. She felt being picked up by Neil's strong muscled arms as he carried her over a few steps. Then she heard a splash. Something had fallen inside the water. She felt cold and wet. Neil had thrown her inside the lake, and she was too weak and dizzy to swim. She was sinking to the bottom. This was it, maybe; the end of her pathetic existence. At least there would be no deceit in death. Just a smooth transition to the other side where she could meet her parents again. She would be safe with them. They were reaching out to her from the other dimension.

But it wasn't meant to be. A pair of hands appeared inside the water and pulled her upwards into the real world.

Epilogue

Constable Badri's wife wasn't amused as he stealthily entered the home, tiptoeing to the kitchen.

'Do you know what time it is?' she asked, standing cross-armed by the door in her nightdress.

'Are the children up?' he asked. Counter-questioning your wife was a bad strategy, a lesson he was yet to learn even after two decades of marriage.

'They slept, after waiting for hours for you, Badri,' she chided him. 'You had to take them to the movies. This is the third time in two weeks that you were not able to keep your promise!'

'I am sorry. I'll make it up to them soon,' he said, sitting cross-legged on the floor. 'I had a case today. A rather enthralling one at that.'

'What case?' she asked, handing him an empty plate. 'You have a case every day. You are a policeman, for god's sake!'

'No, this case was different. Do you remember the disco deaths?' asked Badri.

'That case ended weeks ago,' his wife said, pouring dal in his bowl. 'Who are you trying to fool? It was the obsessed chef who was behind everything! I watch the news. I'm not illiterate like your mother.'

'There is no reason to bring my mother into this, dear,' said Badri meekly, aware that there was ultimately no winning with the missus.

'Tell me about the case,' his wife said, avoiding the topic of her mother-in-law altogether. 'What's new about it?'

'That case did not get over then. There was more to it,' he said, pointing at the empty portion of his plate, an indication to give him a chapati.

'There is no chapati left. I threw your portion to the dogs in anger. You'll have to do with only dal tonight,' she said, nonchalantly. 'Anyway, tell me about the case.'

'So, KK sir had his doubts that there was something about the case that did not make sense even after the saga with that manic chef was over,' said Badri, as his wife poured some dal into his bowl. 'Sameera Kapoor, in her statement, had told him that Chef Alex had implied that he had watched Harsh Kapoor die as he choked on something, and he had also watched Maya Kapoor die of cardiac arrest at the Kapital

Club. KK sir realized that if Chef Alex had actually killed both of them, he would have had no qualms about admitting it to Sameera that night. This fact was further corroborated by a personal diary that we found from Chef Alex's apartment.'

'What's the big deal? Both Harsh and Maya's deaths could be unrelated accidents,' remarked his wife, as she settled down on the floor next to him.

'Could be but that would have been a big coincidence, and in this tale, a mere coincidence didn't seem to be the plausible choice,' said Badri.

'Then what?' she asked.

'Then, we started doing some old-school digging into the individual deaths of Harsh and Maya Kapoor, the parents. We were not able to discover anything new,' said Badri, as he gestured to his wife to put more dal in his bowl.

'We started going over the recent files, and we struck gold when we came across a copy of the passport of Neil Ramamurthy, the American boyfriend from the time he was arrested,' said Badri.

'So, the boyfriend killed the parents?' asked his wife.

'No, my dear. It was his first ever time in India. The parents died years ago.'

'Then?' she asked.

'We discovered that he had listed his mother's maiden name in his passport: Kaveri Singh. It just seemed one coincidence too many,' he said.

'How so?'

'It was a hunch then, but it proved to be right as we dug deeper. Neil's mother, Kaveri was Gyan Singh's sister.'

'Gyan Singh, who?' asked his wife.

'The Kapoor family's most loyal and long-term serving employee of many decades.'

'Oh my god!' remarked the wife. 'I remember now. But didn't Gyan Singh get killed by Chef Alex?'

'Yes, he did,' said Badri, drinking a glass of water. 'And he would have died a hero's death if we hadn't studied this case closely enough. We reached Hauz Khas Village today to bring Neil and his mother in for questioning. But as luck would have it, Neil basically let us catch him red-handed as he attempted to kill Sameera in front of us. His mother and he confessed immediately when we brought them in at the police station.'

'This is so messed up!' she said.

'It is indeed,' agreed Badri. 'Gyan Singh had hatched this plan long back when both Harsh and Maya were alive. He would kill them both individually over the years to avoid any suspicion. He would later give Neil, his nephew in the US, all the necessary information to woo Sameera Kapoor and make her his wife. Without any other relatives, all of Sameera's wealth would automatically become Neil's, and thus his.'

'But how did Gyan Singh kill Harsh and Maya Kapoor? Their deaths were declared as accidents back in the day, right?' asked his wife curiously.

'It was actually a mix of clever planning and a bit of luck, which we learnt through the mother-son's confessions,' explained Badri. 'Gyan Singh slipped a few drops of arsenic, a slow poison usually found in pesticides, into Harsh Kapoor's food, but before the poison could work its wonders, he choked on a bone and died in the presence of Chef Alex. Maya Kapoor was just happy to get rid of her husband. She didn't opt for an autopsy.'

'Oh my! And how did she die herself?' his wife enquired.

'Exactly the same method,' said Badri, presenting his plate forward to her for yet another serving, which was promptly given so that the story continued. 'Gyan Singh had been putting small doses of arsenic in her food for two days before she died. Her body had been a ticking time bomb since then. Luckily for Gyan Singh, the poison kicked in and caused a cardiac arrest when there was a sudden movement to bring in her surprise birthday party. Her death was attributed to her ultra-hectic lifestyle choice.'

'So, that would mean that Neil's mother had no part in this? Only Neil and his uncle, Gyan Singh, are involved?' she asked.

'Quite the opposite,' said Badri. 'The day Neil and Sameera met for the first time in New York City, Sameera's then-date Rohan was stabbed to death in a mugging by two unknown assailants. We are coordinating with the NYPD for the CCTV footage.

Turns out in addition to Neil, the other culprit
was . . .'

'Kaveri Singh!' remarked his wife excitedly,
finishing her husband's sentence.

'100 per cent correct, Dr Watson!'

'But tell me something? How is Sameera? Is she fine
after tonight's ordeal?' she asked.

'She'll live,' said Badri, as he finished the last of
the dal.

Acknowledgements

Okay, so time for my Oscar acceptance speech, most of which I may or may not have prepared even before writing a single word of *Delhi Disco*.

First things first. The odds of my being a writer would have been infinitely low had it not been for Mrs Juliana D'souza, my English teacher at St George's College, Mussoorie. I owe a lot to you for spotting, nurturing and encouraging my love for writing, when I was eleven and all the way until high school. And now, look ma'am, our book is finally here!

This book wouldn't have been possible without my army of people behind me. My mother, my first storyteller and the genesis of everything pure and beautiful in my life. My father, who has believed in me for far longer than I have believed in myself. My brother Siddharth who has been my first reader and my loudest cheerleader since the beginning of time.

Rishabh Goel and Disha Arun Naik, thank you for showing me direction when I needed it the most.

My wonderful, wonderful team at Penguin: Gurveen Chadha and Anushree Kaushal, thank you for taking a monumental gamble on this anonymous author and for believing in *Delhi Disco*. Nikita Dahiya, my editor extraordinaire, thank you for making this book exponentially better with your input and critique. Yash Daiv, thank you for your sage advice and passable humour. Shadab Khan, thank you for churning out this banger of a cover. My sincere thanks to the entire Penguin Random House India team who worked tirelessly behind the scenes to make this book a reality.

My beta readers, Akshit Gupta, Parth Gupta, Ridhi Goel, Nandini Bhatia, Anubhav Joshi, Shubhangi Gupta, Gaadha Aggarwal and Pooja Krishnan, thank you for reading the manuscript in its absolute raw form and providing precious feedback.

Stormy Hazarika, thank you for being contagious about your love for books, Scrabble and conversations over coffee.

Jayesh Balani, Abhishek Singla and Nikhil Sachdeva, thank you for being the most resourceful people I know.

Aadish Jain, Akshay Khanna, Kunal Agarwal, Namrah Nasir and Shubham Agarwal, thank you for being my brothers (and sister) from other mothers.

R. Sandhu, thank you for nagging me into finishing this book. Your constant queries of '*kitne words ho gaye?*' actually helped me reach the finish line.

A huge shoutout to the countless people to whom I reached out, on whose doors I knocked in search of advice, direction or any valuable nugget of information to navigate through the uncharted territory of writing and publishing. Thank you for your time, effort and patience.

A big thank you to you, my reader. I hope you had as much of a blast reading as I did writing *Delhi Disco*.

And finally, a message of hope for all budding writers out there.

Delhi Disco is a sincere effort. And a sincere effort is all you need to get your writing in front of the world. I agree that the journey from conceiving an idea to getting it published can seem overwhelming, but don't lose hope. You are the only champion of your work. If you are looking for a sign that propels you forward, let this be it.

Until next time.

Scan QR code to access the
Penguin Random House India website